Charlotte an[illegible] spot, unable[illegible] aware of them first. She stopped instantly and got up; Meg stared also. Both of them had faces as red as fire. Suddenly Charlotte and Robin were just as embarrassed for having stared.

"I'm so sorry," Lydia said, looking about for something to cover herself up with. "We should have closed the door."

"We shouldn't have stood here staring," Robin began, but for some reason she could not pull herself away. Meg, more in control of the situation, laughed.

"Well then," she said, "why don't the two of you just come in here?"

It was as if the spell had been broken. Lydia, bolstered by her lover's words, got up and brought her guests into the room. She stood before Robin and slowly untied the belt that held her robe together. Charlotte was drawn to Meg, who stayed on the bed, pulled her down, and kissed her hard.

"Sixty-nine is my favorite number," Meg sighed, and Charlotte took the hint right away....

OTHER LINDSAY WELSH TITLES AVAILABLE OR SOON TO BE AVAILABLE FROM BLUE MOON BOOKS:

Circle of Friends
Nasty Persuasions
Necessary Evil
Provincetown Summer / Bad Habits
Victorian Romance

A Circle of Friends

Lindsay Welsh

Blue Moon Books
New York

A Circle of Friends

Published by
Blue Moon Books
An Imprint of Avalon Publishing Group Incorporated
245 West 17th Street, 11th floor
New York, NY 10011-5300

First Blue Moon Books Edition 2005

First Published in 1995 by Rosebud Books

ISBN 1-56201-483-8

9 8 7 6 5 4 3 2 1

Printed in Canada
Distributed by Publishers Group West

A Circle *of Friends*

Chapter One

Ars Amandi

The cork was in a lot tighter than I had expected, and I had to endure some good-natured taunts as I wrapped the napkin around it and turned the bottle slowly, praying that it would not snap off inside the neck. It didn't and eventually I worked it loose and admired the pale wisp that escaped. As Rachel passed the glasses to me, I poured the liquid gold into them, until all eight were filled.

All of the women had one eye on the television, waiting for the ball to begin its descent, watching the sea of people in Times Square sway back and forth as they waited for it as well. It was hoaky, we knew, but we had been doing it for so long that it would have been unthinkable to celebrate without it.

We counted down with it, and at the stroke of twelve there was cheering, followed by kisses, some of them quick and friendly, most of them long and lingering. When that was over, we toasted the New Year. The champagne was as fine as when I had put it away ten years before, for just this occasion.

I stood up and lifted my half-filled glass. "There should be another toast now," I said, and all of the women listened intently. "There should be a toast to us."

"Hear, hear," Robin said, and there were smiles of anticipation all around.

"I remember the day I bought this bottle," I began. "None of you do, because I didn't say anything about it and why I put it away. But after that New Year's Eve ten years ago, when most of us now here got together for a party, I knew in my heart that it would not be the only one, and I knew that this anniversary would come. I wanted something special for it, something that would come through these ten years just as we did.

"This anniversary did arrive, and all of us from that first party are here, as well as some friends we picked up along the way over the years, right up to our newest member. For that, I would like to toast our circle of friends."

All of us drank, deeply, happily, and I could see in their eyes how each was remembering the past decade, what had changed and what had remained the same, lovers gone and lovers found, and through it all, the common thread that bound us all together, some as lovers, all as friends. I looked around at them all myself, so thrilled that I was a part of it. I wanted to honor them all, and thank them all for the friendship I had shared with all and the love I had shared with some.

"To Rachel," I said, beginning with the beautiful woman who sat closest to me, "who became a partner in her firm three years ago, which really came as no surprise to us since she always seems to make a success of anything she sets out to do." She looked especially lovely this night, for her hair, usually pulled back and styled almost severely, was hanging lushly about her face, and those delicious eyes smiled at me over the rim of her glass until I felt weak and giddy.

"To Charlotte," I continued. "Who among us didn't suspect that she and Robin would tie the knot? And to Robin also, who looks like she'll have a second store opened up before we meet again next year." The two women were sitting close together on the couch, and as everyone drank to them, they shared a kiss that was so long and deep it drew kind laughter and some teasing from the others.

"To Margot," I said. "Your own veterinary practice

two years ago and a new house this year—from all of us, a thank you for hiring a moving company and not a moving van that requires seven friends to make it work!" This toast was very well received and Margot laughed; I loved her smile.

"To Astra, and a new gallery opening just a month ago," I continued. "I can't believe you actually came here tonight without a camera in your hand. And to Carly, with an opening of her own."

"And to the first time we've seen her that she's not been covered with paint," Rachel added, and everyone laughed.

"And finally, to Nora," I said, lifting the last sip of wine in my glass. "Our newest member, and a most welcome one. I would suggest that next week you go out and buy a big bottle of champagne and lay it down in your cellar, because in ten years we expect to drink it with you."

"I will," Nora said shyly; she was still new to the group, and not quite confident. That, combined with her willowy body and soft lips made me want to hold her and take her right there, and I knew that sometime in the future, that was exactly what I would do.

On this night, this night that saw us drink wine and play silly board games and talk well into the early hours of the morning, the circle of friends tightened just a little bit closer as all of us celebrated both the coming new year and the fact that we were once again all together. And later on, when the wine was finished and the women, yawning and giddy with sleep, left in twos and threes for the comfort of their own homes, I stood by the door and kissed them good-bye, until only Rachel was left.

"I couldn't take my eyes off you all night," I told her.

"I know," she said, and she took me into her arms and kissed me harder than I could possibly have hoped for.

She was so confident, so sure of every move, and this excited me as much as the feeling of her arms around me and her fingers in my hair. She held me spellbound, and I felt myself drawing power from her lips, from her strong arms about me, from the thighs that rubbed seductively against my skin and made me want that hot, wet haven that waited for me within them.

"You should always start the new year off properly," she said, as she gently bit my neck and carefully pulled down the zipper of my dress. As usual I wore nothing under it, and she worked her way down until I soon felt the soft, familiar touch of her warm lips on my breasts.

Rachel and I shared a most unusual relationship, and just knowing the nature of it was enough to make me needful and hot whenever I thought about it. She treated me as an equal, although I was always aware of her strength and confidence, and it always seemed that she took the lead in our lovemaking, although she did it in such a way that I often felt invited to put my tongue on her clit or my fingers into her steamy tunnel, instead of feeling pushed into doing it. And yet, we both knew that even as we kissed each other and celebrated the beginning of a new year, there was a young woman back at her house, possibly chained by one wrist to the bed, possibly tied to a ring in the wall, perhaps just kneeling on the floor held only by the power of her Mistress's hours-old command. She would be waiting and longing for the moment that her Mistress would unlock the door, even though she was unsure if that return would mean an opportunity to serve or a beating with a leather paddle saved just for that purpose. It might even be two women, or three, or any number of the stable that Rachel commanded as the mood pleased her, and who all but fought each other for the privilege of being first in her Mistress's eyes.

I knew very well the scenes that Rachel would play out with them, sometimes coldly kind, often impossibly cruel. I did not participate in them myself, nor did I look for submissives of my own to control. Instead, I was satisfied to know the power she held over them, and thrilled to know that this power could be mine as well whenever I held her in my arms.

She stepped back, with that mysterious half-smile of hers, and slowly and carefully opened each button on her expensive silk blouse. I couldn't possibly count the number of times I had seen her perfectly shaped globes with their stunning hard nipples, but each time they took my breath away, and this was no exception. My fingers itched to touch them, but Rachel was determined to tempt me further, and she took those firm nubs between her own fingertips and rubbed and tweaked them until they stood out even further.

"You want these, don't you?" she whispered, and I could only nod my head. How badly I wanted to feel that smooth skin under my hands and touch my lips and tongue to them. I wanted to circle them, to suck them into my mouth. I wanted to explore the warm and secretive fold below them where they met her chest, wanted to follow the curve of the muscles that supported them right up to where they blended into her arms. "How much do you want them?" As if she had to ask! She knew that I had longed to touch them all night.

"This much," I said, and I bent down to take her offering. We played this game often, and it always excited me. I knew that she would be just as hot and wet as I was between my legs, and in time I would be there too. I could be patient. We had a whole new year ahead of us.

Those orbs were like sweetest fruit to me, and I savored them until a soft moan of delight escaped my beloved's lips. Once that happened, I could barely contain myself, and the warmth that flooded through me from my crotch was almost overwhelming. Without even being touched, I was as excited as she was and needful in a way I could not even describe.

Rachel stepped back from me, and again with that delicious smile, she removed her clothes with a practiced slipperiness that I had so long admired. She then helped me out of mine, and led me over to the daybed, with its inviting large seat and thick pillows.

She laid me on it, on my back, and when I tried to raise my hands and touch her, she gently but firmly put them at my sides, and told me to relax.

I tried, but it was virtually impossible to ignore the

throbbing that started in my clit and went through my whole body with such ferocity that I could feel my heart pounding in my chest. Who had ever wanted this woman more than I did?

She started at my feet and worked her way up my legs, using her tongue and her fingers to stimulate me, licking and tickling me as she moved. Until I met Rachel, I had only ever thought of sex in its most blatant and obvious ways, in terms of kisses, of lips on breasts, of tongues and fingers on cunts. Rachel taught me that my whole body was sexual, and with her touch she could make the back of my knee or the inside of my arm as sensitive as the hot button between my legs. She was doing this now, and I knew that this orgasm was going to be a killer.

My thighs were on fire when she reached them and she knew it, for she teased me unmercifully with her tongue; each time she got close to the dark hair that shaded my cunt she worked her way around it, so close that I could feel her hot breath, far enough away that I gasped and longed for that first touch like a starving woman. When it arrived, a flick of her tongue over my clit like a wisp, I cried out loud, and Rachel smiled with triumph. Who didn't like to know that she was giving another pleasure? Yet Rachel basked in it more than any woman I had ever seen, and she stretched it out even further by long, slow strokes against the length of my clit, until I didn't think I could bear it any longer. I tried to push my hips closer to that elusive touch, I even held her head and tried to encourage her that way, but she held back, determined to keep me on the edge as long as she possibly could. It was working, for her lips were shiny with my juice, and she licked it off and savored it before returning to that wanting place between my thighs.

Her tongue was featherweight as she flicked it all over me, circling the opening to my tunnel, moving back to my ass, slipping up to roll over both sides of my clit and then to tickle it with just the tip. I was gasping, and my hands found their way to my tits by themselves; it took me a moment to realize that the heat was caused by my own fingers pulling at my nipples to make them even harder. My whole body was responding to Rachel's touch in a way I could not control.

"You like to touch your tits, don't you?" Rachel asked, as she moved back and teased my clit with the tips of her fingers. I nodded; I could not take my hands away from them. "Squeeze them. Make those nipples hard," she said, and I would have obeyed even if I hadn't wanted to, for I was no longer in control. From that place deep between my thighs, Rachel was orchestrating my every move.

When she slipped her fingers inside of me I thought I would faint. A few moments later, she touched the tip of her tongue to my clit and lashed at it, and I exploded into a delicious orgasm.

I was still gasping, my arms heavy and my whole body relaxed, when she knelt over me and presented her own cunt to me. As cool and composed as she always appeared, her flesh was ferociously hot and her vaginal lips were soaked with the juice that I licked away and savored just as she had. The finest brandy could not have been as delightful.

We had experimented with almost every position we could think of, but this was definitely Rachel's favorite, and I suspected it was because she could control what I was doing to her. Sometimes she would lift away from me, or press down harder, or direct my probing tongue and fingers to another place. But no matter what she did, I could always tell when she was close to coming. Her nectar took on a sultry, smoky taste that thrilled me completely, and she ground on my mouth until my whole face was buried in her, and she was everywhere around me.

I could feel the muscles of her thighs tense around me and her whole body was as tight as a plucked string when she finally released. She did not cry out, but I knew that her eyes were tightly closed and her fists clenched, and when I heard her groan, "Ooooh—yes, yes!" in a voice so low it was almost a whisper, I knew that her passion was complete.

Then she was lying on me, stretched out full, and the warmth of her body competed with the warmth of the soft kisses she traded with me. Eventually we stretched out beside each other, and she held me close to her until my head was on her shoulder, her arm circled protectively about me. I could not have been more content.

"A very happy New Year," she said, and it seemed strange to hear that phrase so associated with midnight when the early light of the dawn was coming through the open window blinds.

"To *auld lang syne,*" I said, and kissed her lips softly. I was tired, and as I started to doze off in her arms, I smiled when I realized that before the morning was over she would want to celebrate New Year's Day too.

Chapter Two
Charlotte and Robin

"Open it," Charlotte said.

The box wrapping was almost too pretty to ruin, and Robin admired the cunningly twisted bow and silver paper a moment longer before she unwrapped it. Inside was yet another box, this one long and narrow, and its shape reminded her of something; she caught her breath, hoping that she might be right. She was and she let out a coo of delight when she saw the object nestled in paper inside the box, seemingly waiting for a touch to bring it to glorious life.

"I thought we could have some fun with it," Charlotte told her, and Robin kissed her before she went back to examining the gift.

"That's an understatement," Robin said, taking her birthday gift out of its box. It was a vibrator, almost a foot in length, delightfully thick, made of a soft rubber that felt almost humanly warm in Robin's hands. She ran her fingers over it, her pussy stirring just from the sight of it. "How did you know I wanted one?"

"Because woman doesn't live by hard plastic ones alone," Charlotte said. "Everyone needs a few luxuries in their lives." Her fingers were straying to her lover's thighs, tracing patterns on the stockings and moving slowly up to the hem of her skirt. Once she reached it, Robin spread her legs apart, and Charlotte kissed her deeply while her hand strayed up to that hot area in between. Robin wasn't wearing any underwear and she could feel Charlotte's fingers brush her wiry pubic hair and then tickle at her swollen pussy lips. She moaned, softly, and begged to try the vibrator out right away.

"Oh, no," Charlotte smiled. "We have dinner reservations, remember?"

"Then you should have given me this when we got home!"

"I will," Charlotte promised. "Only now look what

we have to come home to. This way, you can spend the next few hours just thinking about what we'll do when we come back."

Reluctantly, Robin put the vibrator back in its box and got up to get her coat. As she stepped back from the closet, Charlotte came up behind her and pressed hard against her. Robin let herself go limp and leaned back into her lover; she could feel the swell of Charlotte's firm breasts against her spine and imagined she could even feel the heat of Charlotte's pussy through both their skirts. She could definitely feel Charlotte's hands making their way to her tits, to fondle and massage and ignite the fire between her legs.

Charlotte was indeed hot herself, and she wouldn't have been surprised if the heat of her cunt was strong enough to be felt. She loved to touch Robin, loved to see the contrast of her pale skin against Robin's muscular dark body. She loved Robin's small, hard tits and the impossibly ruby red hue of her sweet pussy. She reached down to pull up the hem of Robin's skirt and groaned aloud when her fingers came away wet from the object of her desire. She moved them about as she kissed Robin's neck, listening for the quick intake of breath and the long, soft moan that told her she had hit her mark. She found Robin's huge clit and pressed it back and forth with a fingertip, while another finger gained just the slightest entry into that sweet, deep tunnel.

Robin's body was no longer limp; she was hard, on edge, delighting in the quivers that ran through her body from between her thighs. Her eyes were tightly closed, but her mouth was parted halfway, her breath coming in sharply, escaping in groans of desire and delight. Her hips were now moving, seemingly independent of her, matching the rhythm of the hand that gave her such pleasure. Charlotte was an expert at this, and she could draw feelings out of flesh with an ease that never failed to amaze her lover. But that was unimportant now; the only thing that mattered was that finger on Robin's clit, now wet with nectar, rubbing and trying to coax an orgasm out of that burning cunt.

"You're going to make me come," Robin gasped, her eyes squeezed tightly closed. "It's hot, so hot...ooooh!" She trembled all over at this sweetest release, and when it finally passed completely through her, she was left gasping, once again weak and limp.

Immediately, Charlotte stood up straight and gave Robin a gentle slap on her behind. "Hurry up, we're going to be late," she said, and got her own coat. It was a game she loved to play often; when Robin least expected it, she would hold her, quickly make her come, and then act as if absolutely nothing had happened. Robin laughed and took a moment to calm her breathing before she put on her jacket as well.

The restaurant was Charleston's, Robin's favorite, and one where the two women often met for a drink in the dark, richly paneled lounge after work. The maître d' greeted them warmly and they requested a cocktail before their table was readied. Within moments, they were beside each other in the lounge, sunk into one of the overstuffed couches, watching the hypnotic flames in the fireplace. The hour was still early and they had the room to themselves as they lifted their champagne to toast the occasion.

The wine was like silk, and Robin sat back and admired its color through the glass. "All I can think about is my present," she said quietly. It was the opening Charlotte was waiting for. "All I can think about is how good it's going to look on your sweet pussy," she said. She had deliberately selected a vibrator finished in a light-colored rubber, so that she would be better able to enjoy the contrast between the device and Robin's skin. There was no doubt, this was a present chosen for both of them.

"I can see what will happen when we get home," she continued. "I want to be the one that holds it first. I want to put it on your cunt and make you come. Maybe you'll have on a pair of panties."

"The red ones?" Robin was getting into the game herself, smiling mischievously, sipping at her champagne.

"The red ones will be perfect," Charlotte said. She knew the red panties well; they were silk, cut in a roomy tap-pant style, so that Charlotte could rub the silk on Robin's cunt, or slip them aside effortlessly for a finger or tongue to gain access to the hot flower underneath them. "First, I'll rub the tip of it all over your lips, just to get you wet."

"I'll be soaked," Robin said.

"Soaked through," Charlotte agreed. "Then I'll turn the vibrator on, just a bit, just enough to tease you. You'll beg me to turn it up, but it won't do any good. You'll just have to wait for that."

"It'll feel so good there," Robin said.

"It will look good, too. I'll rub it all up and down your pussy, right through the panties. I'll move it beside your clit, and go right down to your ass just as if it was my finger. After a long rime, I'll take those panties aside and put it right on you, and I know you'll moan out like you always do when I touch you."

"Tell me more," Robin coached.

"I want to put it inside you," Charlotte said. "I want to spread your pussylips with my fingers and put the very tip of that vibrator inside, and then turn it on. I want to hear it buzz up against your sweet pussylips, and I want to see it inside you. That pink rubber will look so nice against your cunt. You know how much I love to see my fingers in there, and this will be just the same." By this time, Robin was obviously excited, and Charlotte looked around quickly. The maître d' and the sommelier were engaged in a quiet discussion, and the waiter was looking the other way. Assured that she was not seen, Charlotte let her hand stray to her companion. As she had expected, the thick hair around Robin's pussy was damp, as subtly as a light mist of dew on a morning meadow.

They finished their champagne and were escorted to their table. The restaurant wasn't very crowded and the closest diners were several tables away. They knew their dinner conversation wouldn't be revolving around the food or their day at work.

They ordered and then sat back with the wine that had been brought for them. Charlotte wasn't letting her lover relax for a moment. "It has a variable speed dial," she said, almost clinically. "I made sure of that, and I made sure to get a spare set of batteries. Do you know what that means?"

"No," Robin whispered, almost dizzy with anticipation.

"I'll be able to drive you crazy with it," Charlotte promised. "I can turn it down and just tickle it across your clit. Then I can turn it to medium and get you all excited. I can just see your hips moving when I have it on your cunt. Then I'll turn it up high, and you'll be at my mercy. I'll make you come again and again. And when the batteries get a little low, I can just pop in a fresh set and send you off again. So what do you think?"

"I think this should be a short dinner," Robin said, although it turned out not to be, for the food was exceptional, and both women appreciated fine dining enough that they would never rush it. Besides, they agreed, the buildup was all part of the excitement.

Robin had ordered her favorite dinner, a thick slice of beef filet smeared with pâté and baked in a crisp phyllo crust. The deep pink interior reminded her of the way Charlotte's pussy looked when she spread the lips with her fingers, ready to apply her tongue to that delightful smoothness. The pâté, highly seasoned, was thick and creamy, and she rolled it on her tongue just as she loved to roll Charlotte's clit between her tongue and her lips, coaxing the waves of pleasure out of it. All of the food was sweet and thickly creamy, the slices of baked sweet potato, the pâté, the spinach baked with cream and eggs. Everything she put into her mouth reminded her of

Charlotte's secretive flower, which she vowed she would unfold later that evening, to their mutual delight.

Somehow they finished their meals, exciting each other with their descriptions and their fantasies, delivered in low tones accented with blown kisses and low moans of delight. Both women were thoroughly enjoying their erotic discussion, even as their pussies throbbed and they sometimes had to squirm on their chairs in their excitement.

"I can't possibly stay through dessert," Robin said, as the waiter noticed their empty plates and hurried to clear them. She was sure that when she stood up the chair would be wet.

"No dessert?" the waiter smiled at her. "On your birthday, Ms. Smythe, you won't be enjoying your favorite cherries jubilee?" Robin thought for just a moment before nodding her assent. For her, fine food was a turn-on, and the sweetly tart dessert would make the whole evening more complete.

The dessert was made at the table, allowing the women to enjoy the sight of the flambé as they sipped their brandy. When the dishes were set before them and the waiter left, Charlotte made sure that Robin saw her tease a firm, red cherry with her tongue before holding it gently between her teeth and closing her lips around it. Robin closed her eyes for a moment and calmed herself before taking a bite of her own dessert. The ice cream was a soft thickness against her tongue, and the cherry popped between her teeth, releasing a spurt of warm, brandy-rich liquid that she savored as if it was Charlotte's honey.

They could hardly wait to get home, and as much as they had enjoyed their long, luxurious dinner, each could feel her pussy throbbing with want as the front door was opened and they stepped inside. The door was barely closed when they were in each other's arms, their tongues reaching to probe each other, their fingers in each other's hair, pressing closer, kissing deeper.

"I can't stand it any more," Robin whispered, and her expensive coat fell in a heap on the floor. Charlotte shrugged hers off her shoulders, her lips still on Robin's, and they left their coats and shoes where they fell and walked arm in arm toward their huge bedroom.

The bed seemed more inviting than it had ever been; the white sheets and the mounds of pillows made them want to stretch out and take each other as quickly as possible. Charlotte sat Robin down on it, and when Robin raised her hands to help with Charlotte's buttons, she was told, "It's your birthday. You just relax and enjoy."

"How can I when my poor pussy's on fire?" Robin asked, squirming on the bedspread to show just how much in need she really was.

"Just think about how good it'll feel when we stoke it a bit more," Charlotte said, and kissed her before standing up straight to take off her clothes.

She did it as a slow striptease, playing with her shirt as she unbuttoned it, caressing the skin that she exposed as each button was released. When the shirt was opened and hanging loose, she pulled the tails up, so that her breasts were lifted with the fabric, framed by the silk. She leaned forward and allowed Robin to lick and suck at them, but just a little before she pulled away again. She massaged her breasts with her own fingers, tweaking the nipples and rolling them between her fingertips, tracing the brown areola with her nails until they were covered with tiny bumps that gave away the height of her excitement. Her breasts glistened with Robin's saliva, her outthrust nipples firm.

Then the shirt was gone, and her fingers sought the waistband of her skirt. Like Robin, she wore no panties under it, and she teased her lover by flashing glimpses of her light brown pubic hair before finally dropping the skirt entirely. She kept on her stockings and garters, and Robin loved the way they framed her pubis and lapped so enticingly at her creamy thighs.

Robin longed to lap there as well, and when Charlotte came close enough, she did. She followed the tops of the stockings with her tongue, licking a circle about them and moving in to slip the tip of her tongue between the tight V of Charlotte's pussy lips. Charlotte moaned softly and stood, trembling very slightly, while the heat and wet of Robin's tongue touched gently at the very tip of her clit, but then she stepped back and said, "Later. Now it's your turn."

She pressed her companion back on the bed and began to undress her, just as slowly and seductively as she had stripped herself, with just as much attention paid to the smooth, dark skin below the fabric. She lingered for a long time on Robin's tits, and when she slipped a hand down to reach below Robin's skirt, she was surprised at how wet that place was. When she removed the skirt, she let her tongue play over the spot, licking the juice away and savoring it, before she stood up and reached for the box on the beside dresser.

Robin had to touch the vibrator when it was revealed, just to feel the rubber, so soft and warm it almost felt like flesh. Charlotte turned it on low, and it buzzed and trembled in her hands....

She used it to massage Robin all over, starting at her throat. Robin could only lie back and revel in the delicious touch of the device. "I always saw them sold this way in magazines," she laughed, as Charlotte rubbed the tip of it around her throat and up and down the back of her neck. "Like they were made just for relaxing a stiff neck. But you know, that does feel pretty good."

"So do you want me to stay up here?" Charlotte teased.

"Not for much longer," Robin smiled. "You know my pussy's just begging for it."

She didn't realize how much she wanted it on her tits until Charlotte worked her way down there. She let it rest ever so gently on the nipples, and the hard brown nubs responded to the vibrating device by becoming firm. "Look how big they are!" Charlotte marveled, and she kept the vibrator on one while she sucked at the other. It seemed to fill her mouth and Robin moaned as she felt her lover's hot, wet tongue tease and tickle at her.

Now the vibrator was on her belly, and Robin held her breath as it moved down lower. When it touched the very tip of her slit, she groaned and exhaled hard. She spread her legs, and Charlotte marveled at how good the pink rubber looked against the ruby flesh. She moved it up and down, still on the low setting, just enough to excite and tease. By the way Robin's vaginal lips gleamed with her honey, the teasing wasn't really necessary, but Charlotte kept it up nevertheless, as much for her own excitement as for Robin's.

They were both almost painfully aware of how much their cunts throbbed with desire and the need for orgasm. Robin was so wet the vibrator slipped inside of her effortlessly, and she gasped as she felt the warm rubber part her lips and fill her with its heft and its movement. She could not believe how good it felt, this dildo that buzzed with a life of its own, as Charlotte moved it in and out.

Then Charlotte took it out, and replaced it with two of her own fingers; while the vibrator danced on Robin's sex-swollen clit, Charlotte fucked her with her hand, until Robin was gasping and moaning, her hips bucking wildly.

She cried loudly as she came with an intensity that surprised them both. The hot sparks went all through her, leaving her trembling in their wake. When they finally passed through her, seeming to escape right from the tips of her fingers and toes, she was left gasping and limp.

"Better than a pair of fuzzy slippers?" Charlotte smiled.

"The best birthday gift I ever received," Robin gasped.

Her whole body felt bare, every nerve end on edge,

ready to receive more pleasure. "But what about you? You have to come too."

"I know," Charlotte said, and she knelt on the bed over Robin's hips. "You think *you* were hot? My whole body's on fire just watching you."

Her pussy was now above Robin's, and she placed herself so they were touching. Robin adored the feel of Charlotte's hair against hers, the burning heat of her lover. Charlotte moved her hips, gently brushing her cunt against Robin's. To Robin's surprise, her own pussy was just as eager as it had been before. Despite the overwhelming orgasm she had enjoyed, she was hungry for more.

Charlotte took up the rubber vibrator, turned it on, and placed it between them.

It slid smoothly in, shiny and damp from Robin's juices. It rested on both their clits and buzzed with a life of its own, affording pleasure to both of them as they lay together.

To Robin it was a tantalizing motion on her sensitive cunt, and slowly the vibrator brought her near a peak again. For Charlotte, it was the first relief that her swollen pussy had felt that evening, and she almost cried out at the first touch. Unable to help herself, she ground her slit on it, trying to touch every part of her to that rubber lover. As she did, she pressed it deeper into Robin's pussy, exciting them both even more.

It didn't take long before both of them were writhing, grinding on the vibrator, gasping and moaning their pleasure to each other. Charlotte's large breasts brushed against Robin's tits, and she reached up and grabbed them, rubbing the pink nipples on her own hard brown ones. Charlotte nodded with delight, hardly able to speak for the moans that the vibrator was coaxing out of her.

She came first, wildly, pushing her hips into the vibrator and crying out as her pussy throbbed out its relief. Within moments, Robin enjoyed her own orgasm, and they sank into each other's arms with the vibrator still between them. It was some time before Charlotte gained the strength to turn it off and take it out from between them.

They stayed like that for some time, until Charlotte moved over to lie beside her lover and wrap her arms tightly around her. "Happy birthday," she whispered.

"I hope we won't just use my gift once a year," Robin smiled.

"I think the day after a birthday is just as important," Charlotte said, "and we'll have to check it to make sure it works properly. Of course, two days after a birthday, gifts should be used too."

Robin started to get up, but Charlotte hugged her even tighter. "Our clothes are still on the floor," Robin protested, but Charlotte silenced her with a firm kiss, slipped off her stockings and garter, and pulled the crisp sheets up over them.

She reached over to turn off the light, running her fingers softly over the rubber vibrator which lay on the bedside table before she did. "You know," she said to Robin, "there are plenty of things you can do before breakfast. You in or out?"

"What do you think?" Robin smiled, snuggling deeper into Charlotte's arms and closing her eyes. With birthday gifts like that, she thought, maybe getting a year older wasn't so bad after all.

Chapter Three

Astra and Margot

It was almost two in the morning when Margot got the call. At first she thought she was dreaming and the ringing was her alarm clock. When she realized what time it was, she reached for the phone, apprehensively, steeling herself for bad news.

It was not. Instead, it was a cold, familiar voice, three tense words. "Come here now." And then a click and the hum of the receiver.

Margot exhaled deeply, and fell back into her pillow. During the night it was as if the bed molded itself to her body, and it was never as comfortable as when she had to get up. Even the pillow was in exactly the right spot. She would have loved to have stayed there, basking in the snugness of the bed and the delicious drowsiness of being half asleep, even for a few minutes longer. But she realized that she was being timed even now, that her caller knew exactly how long it would take her to get dressed and make her way to the place she had been ordered to. And all of that aside, she would get up if only because she had been ordered to do so.

She pushed the covers away and within moments was under the hot spray of the shower. The water woke her up and as she shampooed her thick mane of light brown hair she thought about what was in store. Was there an all-night party in progress that she was being summoned to? Was her caller by herself, sitting up late and thinking of amusing herself at such an hour? Was she in a benevolent mood, or waiting at the door to inflict punishment as soon as it opened?

Thinking about all of the possibilities was too much for her; the hot water that flowed down to her dark pussy almost felt cold alongside the heat of her burning desire. There would be no relief where she was going, and the throbbing was strong enough that she would risk being a minute late. Her mind was moving rapidly, thinking of excuses—the car wouldn't start, maybe a late-night seatbelt or taillight warning from a cop—while she positioned herself in the corner of the bathtub, her legs drawn up, her ass positioned so that her cunt was directly below the faucet.

She pushed in the diverter, and the soft spray of the shower changed to a rush of water from the faucet. Margot put her thumb on the spout and directed the foamy hot spray right at her needful slit.

She gasped at the first touch. The water was warmer than any tongue, and forceful yet gentle as it played on her. She moved her thumb and slid her ass on the slippery tub until her clit was directly under the stream. Her hips moved independently of her, as if a lover's hand was on that fragrant pink flower. She didn't even realize that she had thrown back her head and was groaning aloud.

She teased herself by moving about under the water and directing the flow. She left it on her clit until she was just about to come. Then she moved further back and enjoyed the rush on her hole while she spread her cunt lips away with her fingers. She played it over her tight asshole, enjoying the heat and the liquid sensations there. When she had calmed down a little, she took it back to her clit and built up another high which she tempered by moving back and forth.

When she finally realized she was cutting the time too close, she moved her hot button under the water and stayed there, groaning, watching her legs tremble. She was grasping the faucet so tightly her thumb was sore. It didn't matter; all that mattered was that place between her legs. When she exploded, she cried out loud.

She stood up, somewhat shaky, and turned off the water, then reached for a towel. She was so sensitive that she had to dry her pussy by patting it gently. Even that was enough to make her tremble again.

She ran the hairdryer quickly; there wasn't enough time to dry her thick hair thoroughly. She hastily dressed, turned off the lights, and stepped into the night. After her air-conditioned house, the night was almost oppressively thick and sticky. The streets were almost deserted, and she checked the side streets for police cars as she raced toward the house she had been summoned to.

She parked up the street, as she knew she had to, and walked toward the house. It was an upper-class suburban neighborhood and all of the houses were dark, the night silence broken only by the soft, continuous humming of air conditioners. She smiled to herself. If only these neighbors knew what went on in the house at the corner! But discretion was everything, and no one practiced it as well as the woman who had summoned her. The secret would remain one.

She opened the gate and entered the meticulously kept garden that made up the front yard. Margot was confused; the house was dark. She pushed the bell and could very faintly hear it ring inside. No one answered and she knew better than to press it again. Instead, she stood on the step and waited. She was grateful that the porch and the thick garden made her invisible from the sidewalk, for she knew was not inconceivable that she might have to stand there until dawn, or even later.

As it turned out, she did not. After she had waited for the better part of an hour, the door was opened. She entered and, as the door was closed behind her, immediately sank to her knees on the marble floor.

"Thank you for coming," Astra Tomlinson said. The submissive woman looked up quickly and drew in her breath at the sight of her Mistress standing before her. Beautiful no matter what she wore, Astra was stunning at this early hour of the morning. She wore a black satin corset that hugged her slim waist and accented her hips and breasts with lace. Her milky pale skin and the thick, platinum blonde hair that reached almost to her waist seemed even whiter against her black garment. A satin ribbon, laced down the front of the corset, held it closed. She wore elbow-length black lace gloves and black stockings, and her calves were clad in butter-soft leather boots that Margot knew all so well, for many times she had kissed and licked them clean while lying on the floor. Astra held a riding crop in one hand, and Margot knew it very well too. She had kissed it on many occasions; just as often, it had harshly kissed her. She could have stared at her Mistress for hours and never tired of the sight of her, especially when she was dressed like this, but she knew better, and did not look up again.

She was not fooled by Astra's kindly tone; indeed, it filled her with dread, even more than if her Mistress had been nasty. It was not Astra's way to be kind to her submissives, a fact which Margot had learned all too well over the past few years.

"Stand up," Astra said. Margot obeyed, immediately. "Now take off your clothes."

"Yes, Mistress," Margot whispered, and slipped out of her garments as quickly as possible, leaving them in a heap on the floor. She stood before the tall, imposing woman, her eyes respectfully cast to the floor.

Astra put her hand between Margot's thighs, forcing them apart. Then she touched Margot's pussy, with a gentle touch that was almost loving. Unfortunately, Margot was still very sensitive as a result of her intimacy with the shower taps, and her body gave her away immediately.

"I am glad I did not tell you to take your time getting here," Astra said icily. "You might have stopped for dinner and a movie along the way."

"I am truly sorry, Mistress," Margot said. Her face was almost unbearably hot with embarrassment and she knew how red she was.

"I do not care," Astra said, turning away. Then, before Margot could even see what was coming, she raised her hand, spun about, and slapped the motionless woman hard on the cheek. Margot trembled and almost raised her hand protectively to her face, but at the last moment realized her error and forced her arm to remain at her side. She did not even know she was crying until she drew a ragged breath.

"You are fortunate I am feeling lenient tonight," Astra said. "I might have used the riding crop. But I am willing to be generous. I will even allow you to sleep lying down."

"I am grateful, Mistress," Margot said, and lowered herself to the floor. It was unbelievably hard and cold, made of imported white marble polished to a glassy smoothness. She tried not to think of the bed she had left behind.

Astra motioned to the corner and curtly said, "Come, Eva." To Margot's horror, she realized that a woman had been waiting in the shadows all along, watching. The dark-haired woman, nude except for a leather collar about her neck, did not look at the naked woman on the floor, but quickly crossed the floor and knelt by her Mistress's feet. "I am in the mood for an obedient servant tonight," Astra said.

Then she turned and walked up the staircase, followed by Eva, who took the stairs at a respectful distance behind her Mistress. At the top of the stairs, Astra looked down at Margot, who dropped her eyes immediately. Then the lights were extinguished, and Margot heard footsteps and, finally, the sound of the bedroom door closing.

She could not help the bitter tears that welled up in her and spilled out or the sobs that broke from her throat. There was only her naked body, already bruised by the marble floor, and the tingle on her cheek where her Mistress had struck her. She touched her fingers to her cheek and then kissed them, longing for the morning.

She slept fitfully that night, dozing for a while, waking up shivering, trying to find a way to lie on the floor that didn't hurt. It felt as if she had no protective flesh, just her exposed bones against the heartless stone floor. She wished she could have pulled her clothes over and put them under her as a thin cushion, but she didn't dare.

Mistress Astra had ordered her to lie down nude, and this was how she would have to stay. She was grateful that she had been given permission to lay down. More than once she had been forced to sleep kneeling.

Around 5 A.M.—she had been permitted to keep her wristwatch—she heard a door open upstairs. Slowly, stiffly, Eva came down the staircase, fully dressed, putting on her light jacket. She did not speak to Margot, and the prone woman didn't look at her. Eva left silently, the front door clicking shut behind her. Astra did not come downstairs, and after some time, Margot fell back into a hazy, troubled sleep.

She was awakened with a shock, the tip of a boot roughly in her side. Shocked and dazed, she rolled over and scrambled to her hands and knees. "Forgive me, Mistress! Please, Mistress, pity please!"

Once again, the deceptive concern. "You were given permission to sleep, slave," Astra said. "You have committed no crime." But Margot, her knees aching on the cold floor, knew that there would be repercussions nevertheless.

"Upstairs," Astra said, and Margot stood up to obey. Suddenly her back was on fire, and she realized it was a lash from the riding crop. Twice more the leather stick fell on her soft flesh, and she could see in her mind's eye the hot red welts that would lift from its touch. "I did not say you could walk," Astra commanded.

Biting her lip to keep the tears from falling, Margot crawled up the staircase. Her knees ached worse than she imagined they could have, and even the deep plush of the carpet on the stairs provided little relief.

When she slowed a bit, she was rewarded with another bite of the crop across her exposed ass. At the landing, the command remained in effect, and she crawled along the hallway until they reached the bedroom door.

She knew the room very well, which was fortunate, for as soon as the door closed behind them, Astra put a leather blindfold over her eyes and buckled it tightly at the back of her head, so that while she knew where all of the furniture was, she could see none of it. She could feel the heat build between her legs at the darkness and the musky animal smell of the device, but it was nothing compared to the throbbing that set up once a leather collar was strapped around her neck. Roughly she was raised to her feet by it, pulled a few steps, and then thrown on the bed on her back.

She could feel the riding crop on her legs, and she tensed, waiting to be hit by it any moment. It was removed, and she could picture Astra holding it over her head, debating where it should land. Instead, she felt the handle probing between her legs, silently ordering her to spread her thighs.

She did and then something was rubbed hard against her pussy. She gasped, her hips moving instinctively as the rich sensations went all through her. She was swollen with sex, wanting it, craving a release, but she knew it would not be permitted. She was disappointed when the device was taken away, but not surprised. Instead, she lay panting lightly, wondering what her fate would be this morning.

It was not long in coming, for she felt something touch her lips. "Open," Astra said curtly, and she did so. A ball gag was forced inside and buckled closed around her head. It was then that she knew the instrument that had delighted her so briefly; the ball was permeated with the scent and taste of her own pussy, and she savored it even as her jaw cramped in the unnatural position that the gag forced upon it.

"I suppose you thought that sleeping on the floor was punishment enough for your transgression," Astra said. Her voice was low and slinky, with an edge so icy it sent chills through Margot's nude body. "I can assure you it was not. I told you to come here right away. I can understand you taking time to shower, as I will not accept a slave who is not perfectly clean. The time I allowed for you to get here included the time for you to bathe. However, I did not calculate time for you to give yourself pleasure at my expense, while I was waiting for you. This is a trespass so severe that sleeping on the floor might be considered a luxury compared to what I have planned for you."

At that moment Margot said a silent prayer for the ball gag that forced her mouth open, for she was so filled with remorse that if it had not been in place, she might have confessed her crime and begged forgiveness. As soon as she felt the urge to do so, she realized that if she could have spoken, it would only have compounded the seriousness of her situation. Her whole body was as tight as a string ready to be plucked—she did not know if she was to be bound, or spanked, or beaten with the crop, or thrown to the floor and the lack of sight, the gag in her mouth, the collar on her neck, the knowledge that she was completely under the control and command of this woman who she worshipped was enough to soak her cunt through with hot juice that flowed sufficiently to dampen the insides of her thighs.

Although she could not see, she knew exactly where Astra was, for the floor was made of hardwood and Astra's high-heeled leather boots clicked on them as she walked about. From the sounds, she could tell that her Mistress was at the dresser. Her whole body went first cold, then numb when she heard Astra pull open a drawer. Everything that Astra enjoyed the use of when she was in this room with a submissive was in those drawers: her riding crops, her shackles and gags, her paddles and whips, even those devices Margot dreaded—the leather hoods and the harsh leather straitjackets. She could hear Astra taking something out of the drawer and the sound of the drawer slowly being closed.

"You know what I am doing, don't you?" Astra asked. She paused for a moment. "Don't you?" Another pause. "Are you not going to answer me?"

Margot could feel a thin sweat break out over her body. She tried to whimper, but the ball gag effectively blocked out any noise she tried to make. She knew that she was being baited, and she wondered what punishment would be reserved for such a crime. She heard Astra's boots as the blonde woman crossed the floor to stand beside the bed. Then she felt Astra's strong hands on her, forcing her to turn over, to lie on her stomach.

Her arms were raised over her head, and a leather cuff was cruelly attached to each wrist. They were unfinished leather on the inside, rough and raw. A metal snap was used to hold them together, but not before Margot's hands were placed with the bedpost in between. She was now effectively tied to it, unable to go anywhere.

She could imagine the target she made, with her exposed naked ass and her back waiting for whatever punishment was to be metered out. There was a pause, and then *crack!* as a paddle came down.

By the sound of it, and the searing pain that went through her, Margot knew it was a leather one with its face studded with chrome. She could imagine the way her skin would go deadly white for just a few seconds, and then she could see the waffled red welt that it would lift on her skin. She could imagine Astra's cold smile, the satisfaction she would have once she saw the pain she had inflicted on her submissive.

The paddle came down on her four more times, all in the same place, crossing both her buttocks with each stroke. Margot's ass felt bruised and raw, but she could hardly control her excitement. It was only compounded when Astra put the paddle between her legs and touched her cunt with it. Her body tensed and then quickly convulsed as the icy cold chrome studs brushed against her needy clit.

"Just like an animal," Astra sniffed. "They can't control their urges either." She played on her submissive's clit for a long time, working it with the paddle and then drawing away, until Margot was covered with sweat, breathing hard through her nose—she would have panted had the ball gag not been there—but each time Astra stopped well short of the blessed relief that Margot so craved. Astra smiled. On many occasions she had kept this one on the very edge for as long as she wanted, often an hour or more. Of course, at no time were the slaves permitted the glorious explosion of orgasm. Their reward was never their own pleasure, save for whatever pleasure they received from serving their Mistress's every whim.

Astra loved the sight of the nude woman stretched out on her bed, helplessly attached to the post, blindfolded and wearing a collar around her neck like a dog. It always amazed her that no matter how much punishment she gave to them, they waited like children for Christmas morning, begging for more. When she sent them home she knew they sat watching the telephone, praying that she would call. She did not fully understand their motives or their need to be dominated. What she did understand was her own need to do this to them and the satisfaction it gave her. Of all her stable, Margot was her favorite, and as she ran her fingers over her hot, battered asscheeks, her own pussy stirred. She pressed hard and was rewarded by the tracks of her fingers showing as light red marks on the soft female flesh.

Margot gasped as the cruel fingers dug into her. Raked over her already bruised skin, they left burning designs on her that she longed to see. Of course there was no chance of that, for she was in total darkness from the blindfold. But part of her longing was resolved when those same strong hands grasped her and forced her to roll over on her back, still attached by her hands to the bedpost. Her arms pained her as her wrists spun in the nasty cuffs, and her ass hurt even more as it connected with the bed. But she was being moved by the hands of her Mistress, forced to comply with the blonde woman's wishes, and that was all she wanted.

Those same hands forced her to lift her head from the bed, and the strong fingers unbuckled the gag and roughly pulled the ball from her mouth. She could hear it as it was tossed to the floor. She moved her jaw stiffly and tried to lick her dry lips, which tasted of rubber. She hated the ball gag itself, hated the rubbery smell of it and the way it worked. What she loved was the fact that her Mistress forced her to wear it.

She wondered why she had been permitted the luxury of the ball gag's removal. The answer came quickly as she felt Astra join her on the bed. Then her prayers were answered, as her Mistress's hot pussy moved over her mouth.

She could hardly contain herself, and whispered, "Thank you, Mistress!" before she applied herself to it. Seldom was she granted this ultimate reward, and she could hardly believe her good fortune this morning.

Although she could not see her Mistress's hot slit, she knew exactly what it looked like. Astra's pubic hair was as blonde as her thick mane, so light that she almost looked as if she had none at all. Her pussy was a soft pink that looked almost dark against her fair skin, and she had a huge clit, which Margot now touched with the tip of her tongue. She could feel the tightening as she did so and knew the effect she was having upon her Mistress. It was better than any praise, and she fell to licking and sucking with a passion, hoping against hope that her touch might please her Mistress fully.

It did just that, although Astra would never have made the mistake of letting Margot know. Of all of her stable, Margot was the most skillful at physical pleasure even though she was not aware of it. Astra shuddered ever so slightly as Margot's hot probing tongue touched a particularly sensitive spot, and she moved so that she could be licked all over her blonde crotch.

Margot imagined how good it must look, her Mistress clad in black, kneeling over the shackled and blindfolded slave, having her pleasure whenever she wanted it. In a way she envied the dominatrix; when Margot desired sex, she could only hope for satisfaction and as often as not had only the pleasure of her own hand or her shower. If Astra wanted it, she need only command. But the knowledge that she had been commanded made Margot hot, and she stepped up her efforts.

Her face was wet with Astra's juices, and she wished she could burrow right into the hot tunnel she was licking. Her Mistress was everywhere, her pale thighs touching her, her blonde pussy hair brushing her cheeks, her hot wetness covering her mouth. She breathed in the rich perfume, and her own hot breath went no further than the flesh that pressed against her. She could have stayed there forever.

Astra felt the shivers go through her, hot chills that went right to her spine and out to her skin. She caught her lip and breathed hard as she rode out the orgasm on

Margot's tongue. Of course she did not cry out or even writhe about, for the slave must never know the extent of the pleasure she gave to her tormentor. Still, she stiffened and closed her eyes, and just for a moment gave herself over to the complete release that swept through her like a scarlet wave. When it passed, she breathed deeply, then got up.

"That will do, slave," she said, and Margot would have smiled had she dared. She knew that this constituted lavish praise from her cold Mistress, and she had worked her pussy so well she knew it just had to feel good. Even so, she lay on the bed apprehensively. She was still blindfolded and could not see her Mistress's expression. Even a good performance was often rewarded with a cruel slice from a switch or a slap with a paddle.

She heard Astra moving about, her boots crisp on the hardwood floor. Then she heard the dresser drawer open, and her skin went cold as she wondered what was being removed from it now.

The footsteps came back to the bed, and her wrists were roughly pulled about as the snap joining them was removed. "You may not move them," Astra warned, and Margot remained in her cramped position, with her arms over her head around the bedpost.

She heard the sound of a clock being wound, followed by its loud ticking. "You will remain here as you are," Astra said, "until this indicates that it is time to leave. You will not move your arms nor remove any apparatus until then. Is this clear?"

"Yes, Mistress," Margot said softly. Her voice turned

to a soft moan as she felt Astra's hands on her body. She thrilled to the touch as Astra's fingers traced designs on her body, circling her pussy and moving up to hold her breasts.

She shivered with pleasure as Astra's fingers tweaked her nipples gently, and her pussy throbbed with the touch. Just as abruptly the touch stopped, and she almost screamed. Astra had expertly clipped on a pair of nipple clamps, and their red heat seared through her like a knife.

Her Mistress said not another word, but walked across the room and left, closing the door behind her. Margot could hardly believe the pain. Her chest was on fire from her poor clamped nipples and worse, she had no idea how long she would have to lie there. The timer could be set for a minute or an hour or more.

She breathed hard, swallowing, trying to control the nausea in her stomach. When she was finally over it she lay very still. Even the slightest movement was enough to make the clamps pull on her tits, with the resulting stab of pain. When her breasts started to go numb, she was filled with dread. Taking thc clamps off would be just as painful as putting them on had been.

Still, despite the agony, she lay on the bed, the blindfold in place, her arms numb and cold over her head. As always, she was amazed at the relationship she had with Astra. Socially, they met often within their circle of friends. They even met professionally, for each spring Astra would drop by Margot's veterinary office for her cat's vaccinations.

In professional circumstances, they were doctor and

customer, and Margot never even considered that her superior knowledge of the cat's health put her at an advantage over Astra. Socially, they were friendly and outgoing, no different than any of their other friends. The special nature of their unique relationship was virtually impossible to detect when they were out with any of their other companions.

But if Margot picked up the phone to receive a curt command, or a note was dropped off by a courier, all of that dissolved. Then it was strictly dominant, cruel Mistress and submissive, terrified slave whose only goal was to try to please the woman who would accept nothing less.

Margot did not know why she thrived so in the role and could never have explained why she found herself obliged to carry it out. All she knew was that she was never as excited as when she was kneeling on a hard floor before her Mistress. She often had relationships with other women on an equal basis, but they were physical satisfaction only. The deep sense of achievement that she felt even now, with nipple clamps on her tits and a collar around her neck, could only come from this.

Lost in her reverie, she shifted ever so slightly. It was enough for her breast to move, and she bit her lip firmly to keep from screaming out. For all she knew, Astra might be just outside the door, and it would not do to cry aloud her discomfort. Breathing hard, her eyes squeezed tight behind the blindfold, she slowly brought the pain under control.

Just as she did so, the alarm went off. She started to

relax, but then realized that going limp would also move the horrible clamps.

As slowly as she could, she took her arms away from the bedpost. They were stiff and would not move fluidly. The jerky motion brought another painful reminder from the clamps. She held her breath as she brought her arms down to the point where she could touch the devices. The gentle brush of her fingers as she took hold of them was a white-hot agony.

She knew there was no gentle way to do it, and so she counted to three and sprang both of them at once. The pain flowed over her in waves and she could not help but whimper. Finally, though, it began to subside, and shakily she sat up.

She removed the blindfold and was momentarily blinded by the daylight coming through the windows. Carefully she unbuckled the collar and laid everything neatly on the bedside dresser. She would have liked to have stayed a bit longer, perhaps relished the touch of leather against her throat, but she had to hurry. Her Mistress allowed no tardiness once the alarm had sounded.

Silently she closed the door behind her and walked down the staircase. Like Eva had been earlier that morning, she was stiff and sore. Her clothes were still in a heap and she quickly dressed. Astra did not appear, and once she was finished, Margot closed the door behind her as she left the house.

In the second-floor library, Astra watched through the window as her submissive walked up the street to her car. She noted with satisfaction how slowly and stiffly she moved. The curve of her spine indicated nipples too sore to press against a shirt, and Astra smiled.

Then she stood up, adjusted a garter, and picked up the riding crop from the wine table where she had left it. She knew that the slim redhead would be waiting in the cellar, sitting naked on the cold concrete floor. Her eyes would be wide and frightened at the sound of her Mistress's boots on the stairs.

Astra smiled and closed the library door behind her. If she hurried, she could put her riding crop to good use and still have plenty of time to make her lunch date at one.

Chapter Four

Rachel and Astra

"Astra, I really think this was a great idea," Rachel said to me. "I think so too," I said, dropping my bag on the bed and looking about at the spacious hotel room. I love Chicago, I love everything about this city, and I love this building, which is where I always stay whenever I come out here.

This time was even more special than usual, however. I had invited Rachel to come along. It was a business trip, but I've always firmly believed that you can mix pleasure with work. I had several photo shoots lined up for the next three days, and the editors back in New York were waiting anxiously to see them. Usually I come out here on my own, but when I told Rachel I was scheduled for another trip, she told me she'd only visited Chicago as a stopover on a flight. That was all I needed to hear, and she never even gave it a second thought; just, "Of course!"

I opened the heavy curtains. I liked being on this side of the building, since it faced the Sears Tower. Across the street I could see the rows of offices with the workers bustling about like ants.

The flexibility of my job was one of the reasons why I got into photography. I didn't think I could ever face the grind of getting up every morning, worried I'd be late for my nine o'clock start, and staying in the same room, at the same desk, doing the same tasks over and over, every day until five or six. Right now it was eleven o'clock, and I didn't have to think about anything until the night shoot started around eight. Tomorrow, when those workers were rushing to their desks at nine, I'd be lying in that huge bed with Rachel in my arms, without a single care in the world until the shoot at noon. Then, once the four o'clock session was done, we'd have the whole town to ourselves again until the next morning.

I put my camera bags in the corner—the only disadvantage to this job, for they certainly weighed a ton!—

and went back to the window. The sun was gleaming on the lake and this high up, the traffic noise was almost nonexistent. It felt like we were in our own pleasure room in the sky.

"We're right on the 'Magnificent Mile' here," I said. "The shopping is amazing. You won't believe the clothes—they've got suits here I haven't even seen in New York. Are you in or out?"

I could feel Rachel behind me, and slowly her arms circled me, her hands on my breasts. Her voice was rich and husky in my ear. "Out."

Shopping could definitely wait. I turned to face her and was rewarded with a long, luscious kiss. Her lips were firm and strong, her kiss sweet and forceful, and I met it with a yearning of my own. Perhaps this was why I liked to have other dominatrixes for lovers; there was no bantering, no shyness, just strong desire matched equally kiss for kiss.

I could feel her lift the bottom of my sweater as we kissed and then her hands on my naked tits. Her fingers were refreshingly cool on my skin. Then she pulled the sweater up, until it was bunched on top of my breasts, and she kissed me while she kneaded them.

"Anyone in those offices can see us," I whispered. "Let 'em look," she replied. This was something that had never occurred to me before, but once she said that, I realized it was a very appealing thought. I glanced over, but it didn't seem as if anyone was watching, and as I ran my hands through Rachel's thick dark hair and licked at her throat, I found myself almost hoping that someone would. It felt so deliciously dirty to be standing in front of an open window with another woman's hands on my chest.

Eventually Rachel pulled my sweater off entirely, and then with one smooth movement she bent down, her mouth on my nipples. I drew in my breath for she was amazing. She had a way of rolling her tongue around my tits that left me breathless. She was kneeling now, her mouth still on me, but her hands were working their way up my legs, and I knew my cunt must be wet from the attention she was giving me.

She eased off my skirt with a practiced hand; with her, it was as close to Erica Jong's fictional "zipless fuck" as reality ever could be. With Rachel, it always seemed as if one moment I was clothed and the next I was effortlessly naked. It was a talent I wished I could master, but no matter how much I practiced I was never close to her. Still, it was enough to be with her, be recipient of her extraordinary skill.

I was now completely naked before the window, with Rachel's mouth on my nipples and her hand between my legs. I glanced over at the huge tower and to my delight, I noticed a woman was watching us intently from the window of her office. I told Rachel, who was obviously just as excited about it. "Let's give her something to watch, then," she said.

She stood up, turned and faced the window. The woman got up and walked backwards, her eyes never leaving us, until she reached her office door, which she closed. By her extra movements on the knob I was sure she had locked it. Obviously she did not want to be disturbed by something as mundane as work, when two hot women were making love in front of her!

I was just as spellbound as our voyeur was when Rachel began to take her clothes off. Standing close to the glass so that nothing would be missed, she unbuttoned her shirt and pulled it open so that her delicious globes were uncovered. She put her hands to them and held them forward, as if inviting our guest to touch them. I couldn't resist, and I reached for her, kneading those fleshy orbs until she softly moaned. My own pussy was so richly attuned that a touch there might have sent me off right away.

"Suck on them," Rachel said, and I licked at her left tit and took it into my mouth while she kneaded the right one with her fingers. When I finally finished and stood up, I could see that the woman across the street had her own hands on her breasts, feeling them through her blouse. It made me even hotter.

With her liquid movements, Rachel dropped her skirt to the floor. She was completely naked under it, and I stood behind her and reached around so that my fingers could tickle at the dark patch of hair, so very different from my own blonde hair. I licked at her ear as I watched the woman across the street. One hand remained at her breast, but the other was now slipped down between her legs. I was enthralled, and by the heat and wetness of Rachel's slit, I knew that she was as well.

My fingers came away soaked and I sucked them into my mouth. Her thick nectar was like a sweet, hot liqueur. "Rub me some more," Rachel begged, and I pressed my tits hard into her back as I reached around to touch her. It was a request I was thrilled to fulfill.

Although the building was filled with people, some at desks and some walking around, no one took the time to look at us save the woman in her closed office. I could see that her hand was now down the waistband of her pants, and it was obvious that she was fingering herself as she stood facing us. That was the signal for me to rub Rachel even harder, and I could not believe my own excitement as I pressed her delicious clit back and forth between my fingers.

I slipped my other hand between her legs from behind and gently pressed two fingers into her tunnel. I loved the feeling of it, and it always amazed me how soft it was, yet ringed with such strong muscles. I could feel these muscles tighten about me, and I moved my hand in and out, fucking her with it, while my other hand stayed on her clit and moved it. She was breathing hard now, moaning. Her own hands were on her tits, holding them up almost as an offering to our witness across the street.

The sight of her nipples between her fingers was magical, and I kissed her neck while I continued to work her pussy, one hand on her clit, one hand inside of her soft wet warmth. My thumb reached back to caress the tight rosebud opening of her ass, and she moaned and thrust her buttcheeks saucily at me. They were hot and firm against my skin. I knew she was about to come when her vaginal muscles clamped down hard and tight against my fingers. I caressed her clit, pushing it back and forth and rubbing it, and I could feel her tremble ever so slightly. Then my hand was soaked with her hot juices as she rode my fingers, moaning, taking her complete pleasure from my hands.

Breathing hard, she turned to face me, and kissed me deeply, her tongue pressing firmly into my mouth. I met it with my own, and my cunt was so wanting that I could almost feel my nectar running down my thighs. She knew it too, and standing straight beside me, she cocked her hip and bent one leg forward.

It was perfect for me. I straddled her thigh with my cunt, and moaned as my hot female flesh rubbed against her leg. Our friend across the street was still feeling herself as she watched me move on Rachel's leg, at first slowly, then hard and fast.

It was an amazing feeling, made even better by Rachel's hands on my tits. It seemed like too simple a pleasure, as if it would have been impossible to create such tantalizing feelings just by pressing my pussy against Rachel's legs. But the hot chills shooting from my cunt and making their way all through my body proved that it was true.

The delight was magnified when I looked out the window. Our voyeur now had her slacks pulled completely down, and it was possible to see the dark outline of her cunt when she drew her hand away to show us. It was only for a moment, for she quickly put her fingers back there, giving herself the kind of thrills that I was receiving from rubbing on Rachel. We were strangers, women who would probably never meet, and yet twenty-one stories above a crowded city street we were sharing the most intimate of pleasures. Just knowing that made me even hornier, and I held Rachel to me and kissed her again and again.

Her thigh was wet and slippery from the thick wine that was flowing so copiously from my cunt, and my pussy slid over her skin effortlessly. The heat between my legs was almost unreal and I could feel the familiar sweet buildup in my belly. I needed release, I needed to come! I ground my cunt on Rachel and finally, fucking her leg hard, I exploded in an orgasm that left me shaky.

We looked over. The woman in the window was close herself, and it was easy to tell when she came. She threw her head back, her hand firmly between her legs, and her hips thrust again and again against her fingers.

When it was over, she leaned forward against the windowsill, obviously drained. She stayed there for a long time, before finally standing up straight and blowing us a kiss.

We returned the gesture and watched as she pulled up her slacks, adjusted her blouse, and straightened her hair. Then we watched as she opened the door to her office and went back to sit at her desk. Very shortly someone came in to speak to her, and we couldn't help but smile. If only he knew! But she was all business again, and he never looked over to see two women naked in each other's arms. Finally we drew the curtains.

"Fabulous shopping, you say?" Rachel smiled.

"Beyond belief," I told her, and she picked up her clothes and began to dress. For Rachel, sex was almost everything, but now that she had enjoyed one pleasure, it was time to give in to her second-greatest joy.

The shoot was going very well, or at least it seemed to be from Astra's point of view. When things were smooth as they were here, it was a joy to watch her work.

We went shopping after our charming episode in front of the window at the hotel. I thought that I would be completely satisfied, following my experience with Astra's fingers, but as soon as I put on my clothes, the touch of the silk on my skin was enough to set me off again, and I walked through the hallway to the elevator almost in a state of sexual euphoria. How wonderful it is to be a sensual woman!

I had never been a tourist in Chicago before and as we stepped out onto the sidewalk, I was glad that Astra had invited me along and amazed that I had never thought to visit here before on my own.

The city's architecture fascinated me once Astra told me to look up, for most of the fancywork and gargoyles were located high up on the buildings. I'm afraid I gawked like a tourist, to the point where Astra grabbed my arm to keep me from walking into traffic.

It was the stores she had lured me with, and she wasn't lying about them, as I quickly discovered. We ended up in several of them, and very shortly I found myself laden with bags and charging a small fortune as I went through racks of clothes I couldn't resist.

One in particular caught my eye, a very tiny miniskirt made of thin, buttery-soft black leather. It would have been interesting on its own, but it had the benefit of a heavy chrome-laden belt and a slit in the side that went almost up to the waistband. I tried it on, and when I came out of the fitting room to see the mirror, I noticed that the clerk caught her breath at the sight and then dropped her eyes quickly. Her motions weren't lost on Astra either, and both of us smiled at each other. We would remember this sweet little blonde woman—after all, we were in Chicago for three days!

Of course I ended up buying the skirt, along with a leather bolo decorated with the same chrome embellishments. The Versace dress and the silk lounging suit would be kept for business and social engagements, but the slit skirt, along with fishnet or black stockings and black boots, and the bolo with nothing worn under it, would be reserved for standing in front of a naughty young woman in need of some discipline. As I paid for it—glancing at the clerk, who once again stared down at the desk—I could hardly wait to put it to use.

Once we were done shopping, we dropped our packages at the hotel desk and had the doorman call a cab for us. Our first meal in Chicago was a special occasion, and we enjoyed an early dinner in one of the city's older restaurants, a rich, dark, comfortable room where the service was superb, the food excellent, and our table secluded enough that halfway through dessert I reached under it and played my fingers on Astra's thighs until she closed her eyes and pleaded for mercy.

By six-thirty, we were at the location, and Astra was ready to set up so that they could begin at eight.

Unlike some photographers, she was not content to show up at the appointed time; she liked to arrive early and make sure everything was to her satisfaction. It was amazing to watch her—there was a whole crew at the site, including several people from the advertising agency who were responsible for the shoot, but it was Astra who dominated everything. Lights were moved a fraction of an inch, props were brought in or taken away all at a movement of her hand or a single word from her lips. When the models were ready, it was she who decided where they would stand and what they would do. Some of them had worked with her before, and they were obviously in awe of her. Those who were new to her shoots learned quickly enough who was in charge of the entire operation, if not officially, at least in practice.

She shot some Polaroid pictures as a final check, and then the actual work began. Her energy and professionalism were glorious to watch, as she knelt to get a shot from below, stood on a box to get one from above.

The client was, of all things, an Irish-whiskey distiller, and Astra's plan was to show a professional couple, obviously just finished a hard day's work at the office, letting loose on their way to enjoy the Chicago nightlife. The advertisers wanted the product in the picture, and at first Astra took several rolls of film this way, but eventually she convinced them that the campaign would be even more powerful if only the suggestion of the drink was involved. Anyone else might have been laughed off or put down for her comments, but Astra wasn't just anyone, and the executives listened and finally went for her idea. Astra took the bottle and the glasses away and positioned the models as she saw best, this time with absolutely no comment from anyone. As it later turned out, it was this series of shots that made it into the magazines, and the company's sales moved accordingly.

At ten-thirty, Astra decided that she had enough pictures, and the lights were put away, the crew breaking up. The heavy camera bags were loaded into a car, and one of the advertisers gave us a ride back to our hotel.

The bags were entrusted to the hotel desk, to be delivered upstairs, and Astra steered both of us into the hotel lounge, where she ordered drinks for both of us. "That went better than I thought it would," she said, as she relaxed into the comfortable chair across from me.

"I was surprised that they listened to you," I said. "I always thought their ideas were carved in stone and the photographers had to go along with them."

Astra smiled, and took a sip of her drink—a brand in direct competition with the company she had just worked for, I noticed with amusement. "Those people just need someone to tell them what to do," she said. "If you go up to them and say, 'Please, won't you listen to my idea, Mr. Executive?' they'll walk all over you. The key is to let them know who's really the boss right from the start." She lowered her voice and looked at me with a rich, smoky glance that sent a thrill through me. "Just the way you let a little bitch know, when you put a collar around her neck and order her to put her wrists out so you can put cuffs on them. It's all the same, just without the riding crop."

"A nice way to put it," I said, smiling.

"Of course, once they take those pictures back to the office, the client will go on about what a great idea it was to take the product out of the shots," Astra continued. "That's when they'll sit there and say it was all their idea. Now that's when I'd like to have the riding crop handy!"

"I can just imagine you using it, too," I whispered. "Right across their bare asses, until they're all shiny and red—"

"Oh, Rachel, finish up your drink and let's go upstairs!"

I did and we made our way to the elevators. Upstairs, our bed had been turned down, with chocolates and two small bottles of cognac left for us. Astra undressed me and laid me down on those inviting sheets, then took off her own clothes. I admired her body, as I always did: Her skin was so pale, her nipples and lips such a light pink, that I always had to contrast it against my dark hair and olive skin.

She had a small embroidered bag beside her suitcase, and she went into it, drawing out the treasure she had stashed inside. It was a large dildo, thick and fleshy, attached to a leather harness meant to go around her waist and strap securely between her thighs. I knew the type of device well. I even owned one and had used it for cruelty on my submissives, but the thought of using one with Astra, for pleasure only, had never occurred to me. Seeing it in her hands, watching her caress its length and run the straps through her fingers, I didn't know why I hadn't used it that way before myself.

She used it as a dildo on herself first, standing with her legs spread wide apart, rubbing her hot cunt with its head, and then moving the whole length of it so that it pushed between her pussylips and emerged shiny with the juices of her hot excitement. I watched her position it at the front of her soft mound, the hard masculine object emerging from the sweet feminine flesh. When she buckled it around her, the black straps looked delightful against the whiteness of her skin. She paraded with it, stroking it back and forth, jerking it, using her fingers to manipulate the rubber head. My crotch was hot from watching her, and she knew it. She played with it for both her enjoyment and mine.

Then she came around to the head of the bed and put the device invitingly in front of me. "Suck my dick," she said, and I almost felt a need to take it into my mouth. It had a rubbery taste, but it was covered with her sweet pussyjuice, and I eagerly licked and sucked at it to get every last drop of it from the device.

She smiled at me and moved her hips slowly, rubbing it against my lips. "You look so good doing that," she said. "I like having my cock sucked." I was only too happy to oblige, and followed it up by touching her sodden pussy with my fingers while I did so. She moaned, making me want her even more.

With the cock gleaming and wet, she went to the foot of the bed and crawled onto it. I spread my legs wide, waiting for her, and I held her to me as she crouched down over me. I could feel the head of the cock at the opening to my cunt, and I kissed her hard as I welcomed it inside.

She pressed it into me slowly, firmly, smoothly, and I could feel it fill me until her belly was right on mine. "Fuck me," I told her, and she did, slowly and gently, until my urge was so great that I pushed my hips up to meet her.

"Harder!" I urged, and she ground into me, slamming that cock deep into my cunt. I grabbed her ass-cheeks and pulled her into me, pushed her away, rammed her back into me. Our tits were mashed together, our breath coming hard, our bodies gleaming with sweat. Astra reached behind her, putting her finger on her clit, jamming her hand against it so that both of us were in ecstasy.

She came before I did, and as she trembled and cried out, she continued to ram the cock into me. I exploded myself, holding her tightly and moving my hips to get every last ounce of pleasure. Then we lay together, her weight warm and comforting on top of me, my pussy still throbbing with the dildo inside.

It was so nice in the soft bed that we didn't get up again, but put the dildo on the bedside table, ate the chocolates, and emptied the little cognac bottles into the glasses thoughtfully left with them. Astra told me that she didn't have to be anywhere before eleven, so I picked up the telephone and ordered our breakfasts to be brought up by room service in the morning. Then she asked if I would wear the dildo when we woke up. I told her I wouldn't consider anything less.

Chapter Five

Introductions

"I've never done anything like this before," Laura said shyly.

"There's always a first time for everything," Janice told her confidently.

The music in the background, probably from the stereo on the shelf, was instrumental, with a heavy beat. Janice reached up to lift the silk shirt gently off Laura's shoulders. Underneath, Laura was wearing a wickedly sexy corset, red satin with black lace trim, not at all in keeping with her demure hesitation. It showed off her magnificent tits, pushed up over the wire foundation of the bra until the nipples were exposed. When Janice helped her off with her skirt, she was wearing only a tiny G-string under it, a scrap of black fabric that went enticingly up the crack of her firm, smooth ass, a G-string which they both worked to remove. She left on her high-heeled shoes and the corset, arranged her hair down over her shoulders, and licked her lips.

Janice kissed her, at first gently and then with a growing passion. Laura met her kisses and moaned as she felt the first touch of Janice's fingers brushing against her exposed pink nipples. Laura laid back on the pillow and Janice took off her own clothes. Under her business suit she also wore exotic lingerie, which she left on along with her high-heeled shoes. It was an outfit which left her crotch bare, and Laura reached out as if she wanted to touch it. "You have such a beautiful pussy," she said.

"Yours is lovely, too," Janice said. "It's all wet. See, you've wanted a woman all along." Then she kneeled on the bed and took Laura's tit into her mouth.

"It isn't so bad, is it?" she asked.

"No," Laura gasped. "It's better than I thought it would be. Oh, eat my cunt, Janice, I can't wait to have a woman there!"

Janice obliged immediately. She closed her eyes and sighed happily as she put her mouth to Laura's pussy and buried her face in it. Her fingers went between her own legs to manipulate her clit, her pussylips shining with her thick sweet fluid, as she licked her companion with a fierce ambition.

"It's so good!" Laura sighed, and began to roll her own nipples between her fingers. She was moaning almost constantly and every now and again she lifted her head off the pillow, looked down at Janice, and then threw her head back wildly and groaned some more. Janice arranged her hair behind her head and fell back to licking, stopping only to insert two fingers into Janice's pussy and move them slowly in and out.

"More! More!" Laura gasped—and then the screen went dark when Nora Stevens hit the button on the remote control to move the videotape to another scene.

She sighed and slumped into the corner of the sofa, watching the counter spin rapidly on the television screen. This particular film had a pretty corny plot, but some of the sex scenes were very hot and best of all, it was all women.

Nora loved watching women make love. She loved watching them on videotape and she loved looking at photos in magazines. She loved reading about women loving women. The thought of having a woman kiss her and make love to her, of putting her tongue to a woman's soft pussy and licking and sucking until she came, made her incredibly hot and wet between her legs. The only problem was that it was only a fantasy.

She stopped the tape, watched it for a moment, and

then hit the fast-forward again. She was very horny and she wanted to make herself come, but she also wanted to do it while watching her favorite episode on this particular tape.

She thought about women while she watched the actresses on the screen go through their motions at the wildly exaggerated pace dictated by the speed of the tape. No other kind of sex appealed to her the way lesbian sex did, and nothing else made her as excited. The problem was that while she desperately wanted to satisfy this craving, she hadn't a clue as to how to go about doing it.

Finding men who were outspokenly attracted to her slim figure, her blonde hair, her nicely sized tits, and her radiantly blue eyes was relatively easy, but finding women who came on to her wasn't quite the same thing. She thought about going to a gay bar, but she didn't know of any, and didn't know anyone she could ask. Each day she read the personals column of her local newspaper, her eyes searching the page until she found the "Women Seeking Women" section. She read every ad completely through, surprised at the large number that appeared in each edition. Each day she made a mental game of it, shopping through them, eliminating the ones outside of her age range, choosing between the ones that appealed to her, until she finally found one that she thought she would like to answer.

She never did, although she did come so close that she actually picked up the phone and dialed one of the numbers, her heart pounding like a jackhammer, but she hung up after it rang twice. She wanted it desperately, but she was just too nervous to go through with it.

She wasn't even sure if she'd recognize a come-on if she received one—in fact, she wasn't even sure she knew what a lesbian looked like! She knew the movies she watched were nothing but voyeur fantasies acted out by actresses, and she knew that the film stereotype of the woman with teased blonde hair and blue-shadowed eyes—who kept her high-heeled shoes on in bed!—was just that. But did real lesbians look like she did, like the close-cropped women she saw on magazine covers, like the activists that marched in the Gay Pride parades? How would she know if a woman standing in front of her wanted Nora as much as Nora wanted her?

She thought she had been approached, but it was too subtle for her to be sure, and of course there was no way she could possibly ask what the woman's intentions were! Nora was a book illustrator and several times she had done work for an advertising agency where she always dealt with a woman named Charlotte West. She'd heard rumors that Charlotte was gay, that she was even married to another woman, but the stories had never been substantiated. Still, she felt like Charlotte had looked her up and down the way the men did, and once she had invited Nora to come out for a drink after work. Nora had had a deadline that day and had to refuse. The job almost didn't get done on time, for instead of concentrating on her work, Nora could only think about the possibilities, wondering beyond hope if the request for a drink had been just that or if she had been approached for something more. The fantasy that ran through her mind was so strong that she had to stop halfway through and obtain relief for her throbbing pussy with her fingers.

The tape counter reached the number she had been looking for, and she pressed the button to run the tape at normal speed. On the screen, two women returned to their hotel room after shopping, one of them complaining about how horny she was. Within moments, both were completely nude with their arms around each other.

Nora reached into the drawer of the table beside her and drew out a vibrator. Her eyes never leaving the screen, she pulled up the caftan she wore, revealing her blonde pussy. She was always amazed at how hot this particular scene made her, and without turning the vibrator on she rubbed it over her clit, shivering gently as she did so.

It was obvious the women were enjoying what they were doing, for they made love with a relish, giggling like schoolgirls at the joy of having each other. Nora was envious of them, and imagined herself beside them, turning a couple into a threesome. She wanted to touch the dark woman's breasts just as the redheaded woman was doing. She wanted to feel the warmth and the fullness with her fingers.

She turned the dial of the vibrator just a little, so that the plastic device buzzed gently against her sex-swollen clit. She liked to move it slowly, to build up to a dazzling climax just as the women on the screen came themselves. She had done it so many times to this particular tape that it was as carefully choreographed as a dance, and just as beautiful and satisfying. "Let me lick your pussy," the redhead said on the screen, and Nora whispered "Yes, yes, please!" even though she was barely aware that she did so. All she wanted was that dark woman's crotch next to her face, so that she could stretch out a probing tongue and lick the wetness away from the full lips, then stretch them wide and apply herself to that huge nub that waited inside for attention.

The women on the screen arranged themselves on the bed, the tall, dark woman on her back, the smaller redheaded woman settling herself over her. They were now cunt-to-mouth, and Nora sighed, for there was nothing she found as hot as a sixty-nine, and the camera made the most of this one. The vibrator was turned up a couple of notches, and she gasped as it sent thrills through her whole body from that hot, wet place between her legs.

The redhead's tongue probed at the darker woman's pussy, which had been shaved except for a small patch at the rise of her belly. Her cunt was naked, shining with the juices of her wanting, and Nora could see everything as the woman on top reached down with her tongue.

The tip of it seemed to slide into the triangle of her pussylips and almost disappear inside as it swept over the huge clit. Nora shivered. She wanted someone's tongue to touch her like that, and she longed to be able to part someone else's pussylips with hers and give them the thrill that she knew she could.

She didn't even realize she had stuck her own tongue

out, as she moved the vibrator faster over her aching slit. She reached with it, as if she was licking upwards as the darker woman was doing, pulling her lover's asscheeks down so that she could bury her face in female flesh. Nora moaned and pulled the vibrator hard into her. When the camera showed both women, writhing and moaning, she turned it up as far as it would go and held it firmly against her clit.

Her whole body shook convulsively as she came, and she threw back her head and cried out loud as she did. When she was finished, she put the vibrator to her lips and licked the rich hot juice from it. She loved the taste of her own pussy, and she wondered if she would ever have the chance to taste another.

The next afternoon, she was invited again to have a drink with Charlotte West. Her heart pounding, her mouth dry, she whispered yes.

"This is Robin Smythe," Charlotte said. "I don't believe you've met."

Nora stood up from her chair and shook Robin's hand. She was still a little nervous—although a bit less now that she had finished her first drink—but now her main emotion was disappointment. If she had suspected even slightly that Charlotte was coming on to her, if she had hoped against hope that something might happen, the presence of this beautiful, tall, slim black woman, obviously invited to the bar by Charlotte, dispelled any chance of anything happening.

"I understand you're an illustrator," Robin said.

"I do books, yes," Nora said, as she accepted her second drink. "Recently I've been doing drawings for magazine advertisements as well, and that's how I met Charlotte. And you?"

"I have a clothing store," Robin said.

Nora sipped her drink. "Is that how you know Charlotte? She shops at your store?"

She couldn't miss the questioning look that Robin gave Charlotte, and she was confused. Had she said something wrong?

"Robin and I live together," Charlotte said. "I'm sorry, I thought you knew."

"Oh, roommates," Nora said. "I shared a house that way in college. It certainly kept the costs down."

"No," Charlotte said. "We're not roommates, we're lovers."

For a moment Nora didn't know what to say. It was a bit of a shock—she hadn't believed she'd ever meet real lesbians after all her years of watching her fantasies on screen. At the same time, she couldn't believe her fortune.

"I hope it doesn't shock you," Robin said.

"Oh—of course not," Nora said. Then, just a little giddy from the news and her drink, she blurted, "I always wanted to meet someone like you." She couldn't believe she had said it, but at the same time, she saw the look that passed between the two women. She drew in her breath as their eyes met.

They sat for the longest time, making small talk until Nora thought that she would explode. Finally she could hold it no longer, and she said, "Charlotte, I appreciate your thoughtfulness, and I'm enjoying myself very much, but why did the two of you ask me to come for a drink?"

The two women looked at each other for several seconds, until finally Robin leaned forward and said quietly, "We thought you might like to come up for a nightcap later. At our house."

Nora was almost in a daze as they finished their drinks and Charlotte got a cab for them. Even when she was sitting in their living room, being offered a snifter of finest brandy, she still felt as if she were watching a movie of three other people sitting and talking. It was just too hard to believe that it was really happening to her.

She was still in this dreamy state when Charlotte came over to sit beside her, and she felt a hand on her leg, moving slowly and smoothly to caress her thigh. Charlotte's voice was warm and low in her ear. "We thought you might be the sort of woman for this," she said. "Were we correct? Is this what you want too?"

Nora smiled, and it only seemed real when she put her hand down and set it over Charlotte's warm fingers. "I've never done this before," she admitted.

Charlotte withdrew her hand, and apologized, but Nora, shocked at her own forthrightness, reached over and took the hand, putting it back on her own leg. "No, please," she said, looking at both of them. "I've never done this, but I want to, please! This is what I've always wanted, always!"

The two women looked at each other again, and Nora immediately understood the unspoken language they shared, as Robin came over to sit beside her and take her brandy glass away. It was still happening as if in a dream, for it was almost beyond comprehension that after all those years of watching videos and wishing, it was finally going to happen.

She hardly even felt the buttons of her shirt being opened, but she definitely knew when Charlotte's fingers found her breasts and stroked them as softly as a whisper. Her whole body reacted to it, and she looked down and saw her nipples standing out, hard and wanting. The sight of Robin's dark skin on hers was rich and comforting, lovely to look at. She leaned back into the sofa and let the two women feel her breasts. The warmth that went through her whole body was almost indescribable.

They undressed her slowly, running their hands over her long legs and commenting on the blondness of her sweet cunt.

Then Charlotte took her hand and helped her up off the sofa. "Come in the bedroom, it's much more comfortable," she said. Robin was slowly running her hands over Nora's back, cupping the tight swell of her ass-cheeks. "I remember my first time. I want it to be as nice for you."

The bedroom was quite different from what Nora was expecting as well. In all the movies she had seen, the bedrooms were usually either overdone or just a bed on a cheap set. The room that Charlotte and Robin shared was very tastefully decorated, the furniture heavy and well made, the bed inviting with fluffy pillows and a spotless white duvet. The feather comforter was warm and gently yielding as she sat down on it.

The women undressed each other in front of her and then sat down on either side of her, naked. Nora couldn't help but stare at them. She was intrigued by Charlotte's delicious tits, by the wiry dark hair on Robin's pussy. She wanted to touch them both so badly that her very fingers felt hungry for them, but even though she was sitting completely undressed between them, she was too shy.

"You say you've never had a woman before," Robin said. "How do you know that you want us?"

Nora loved the look of her dark nipples. "I've always wanted a woman, as long as I can remember," she said. "I watch women in movies and I want to touch them and lick them. I've wanted it so badly that I can't believe this is happening."

"Believe it," Robin said, and put her lips to Nora's and kissed her hard. It was the first of many touches Nora had been waiting for. Robin's lips were soft and full and so delightfully warm against hers, and when she pressed her tongue to Nora, the blonde woman took it and met it with her own. As she kissed Robin, a long lingering one that Nora thought might never end, Charlotte was reaching over to caress her body. The touch of the brunette woman's hands on her arms, on her shoulders, teasing her nipples, was amazing.

"I can hardly wait to taste you," she begged when Robin finally leaned back.

"There's time enough for everything," the black woman said. "I don't know about you, but we have all night."

"All night's just fine with me," Nora said, and she

submitted to the pressure of Charlotte's hands inviting her to lie back on the bed.

She was still a bit nervous, and the two women spent a long time helping her to relax. They ran their hands all over her, giving as much time to her arms and legs as they did to her breasts and the thin, light hair that adorned her pussy, until she lay back, soaking it all up and moaning softly at the touch of their fingers. Finally Robin leaned down and parted her legs gently, then flicked her tongue against Nora's hard, aching clit.

Nora's whole body trembled at the touch and she moaned out loud. She had had her clit touched many times before, as often as not by her own hand or her vibrator, and each time it was a delightful rush throughout her whole body. But when she looked down and saw Robin's face between her legs, licking her, while Charlotte's hands played with her tits, it was as if she was a virgin experiencing sex for the first time in her life. Never had anything felt so good.

Robin moved very slowly over Nora's cunt, licking everything she possibly could. She ran her tongue into the place where Nora's legs curved into the sides of her pussy, and up her thighs. She moved down to lick at Nora's tight ass, pulling her cheeks gently apart with her hands and kneading them with her fingers as she did. She made long laps on Nora's vaginal lips, and made a point of her tongue so that she could slip the tip of it into the entrance to Nora's hot, soaking tunnel. Everything she did seemed to feel better than the last, and Nora moaned loudly.

"Would you like to try me now?" Charlotte whispered, and Nora nodded. She didn't even realize that the tip of her own tongue was pushed between her lips, as it always was when she watched the films on television, longing to touch it to female flesh. She didn't even trust her voice when Charlotte asked; it was enough that her fantasy was coming true.

Charlotte climbed up on the bed and knelt over Nora's face. At first, Nora did nothing but stare and breathe deeply. She couldn't get over how beautiful Charlotte's cunt was and how good it smelled, so hot and ready, so in need of a tongue to relieve the pressure built up inside. No movie or photo had come even close to capturing the reality of Charlotte's pussy suspended so close over her face. Before she even touched it, she knew that this was going to be a rare experience, one that lived up to the expectations of her fantasy.

Hardly daring to breathe, she reached up and held Charlotte's strong thighs with her hands and pulled that gorgeous pussy down so that she could reach it with her mouth. She touched it with her tongue. The taste was delicious and she savored it, the heat was almost unbelievable. Charlotte didn't rush her, but was content to hold herself there, enjoying the feeling as Nora's tongue touched her at first shyly, then with growing confidence and desire. Now it was time for Charlotte to move on Nora's tongue, and she did, slowly, sensually, reaching down with her hands to hold Nora's tits and massage the nipples between her fingers.

"It looks so good from here," Charlotte said. Robin smiled up at her, then went back to sucking Nora's blonde pussy. "Nora, your tongue feels great on my cunt," Charlotte continued. "That's it, that's my clit. Lick it, lick it hard! Just like that!"

Nora needed no encouragement at this point. She didn't think her tongue could move that fast, but Charlotte's obvious enjoyment, combined with the effect that Robin was having on her cunt, was driving her wild. She found the hard nub of Charlotte's clit and homed in on it. It felt deliciously hot and wet on her tongue, slippery from the sweet juice of Charlotte's pussy. The taste and the heat were better than she had ever imagined in her wildest fantasies. She pulled Charlotte close to her, and when Charlotte ground her pussy against Nora's tongue, the blonde woman went almost crazy with desire for more.

This was what she was meant to do! The black woman's mouth on her cunt was thrilling her, but having her own tongue on another's clit was just as exciting. Her tits felt deliciously full, almost throbbing, at the touch of Charlotte's hands on them. She was close to coming, but her two lovers realized it, and when they moved away from her, she gasped and moaned.

"Take it easy," Robin whispered to her, as she moved up from between Nora's thighs to lie on top of her and softly kiss her. "We have the whole night to ourselves. This is only the beginning." She mashed her tits into Nora's, and Charlotte used her fingers to feel both of the women, the rich dark brown tits and the pale white ones, their nipples touching, turning each other on.

After several more sensual kisses, Robin got up, and

she and Charlotte had Nora stand up. They spent a long time running their hands over her, and Nora groaned as she felt Charlotte's fingers part her pussylips and slowly rub the clit between them, so desirous and so close to coming that she felt weak. When Charlotte finally took her hand away, she put it to Nora's mouth, and Nora was rewarded with the taste of her own steamy pussy on Charlotte's fingers. She sucked them eagerly, slipping her own hand between Charlotte's legs to touch her there. It felt as natural as anything she could imagine, and it only turned her on more when Robin insisted on licking the thick, sweet nectar from her hand. Then the black woman kissed her, and when she probed with her tongue, they shared the pussyjuice together in their mouths, moaning softly, their cunts on fire.

Now the two women knelt on the floor beside Nora, Charlotte in front of her and Robin behind, and gently they positioned her feet so that her thighs were apart, her slit bared to them. Each took her place. Charlotte licked at Nora's pussy, while Robin used her fingers and her tongue to explore the hot rosebud of Nora's ass. Even though Robin had licked her there before, Nora was still new to the experience and a bit hesitant. She clenched her muscles at the first touch of Robin's tongue, but when she forced herself to relax, she realized that it was unlike anything she had ever enjoyed before, hot and delightfully wicked, and within moments she was begging Robin to explore deeper.

Both Charlotte and Robin were eager to respond to her plea, and they licked at her with a renewed passion, fueled by the fact that they had reached under her and had their hands in each other's cunts even as they gave pleasure to the third woman between them. When Nora saw this she put her head back and moaned out loud. While the reality had finally hit her—the fact that it was true, that two beautiful women were making love to her and she to them!—it was still the culmination of her fantasy, and she was drinking in every moment of it. She could almost feel the hot, slick juice on her fingers, and she could see Robin's dark hand shine with the sweet liquid from Charlotte's crotch.

They were bathing her with their tongues, exploring every crevice, and when Charlotte slipped two fingers into Nora's soaked hole, she was filled completely. Fingers in her ass, fingers in her cunt, tongues exploring and licking, harder, stronger, faster, and then she came, her whole body going hot as fire, the orgasm racing through her and leaving her breathless.

She had to sit on the bed, afraid that she might collapse, for her bones had all but melted away. Charlotte and Robin were on her in a moment, prolonging the ecstasy by caressing every inch of her body with their hands. When she could finally speak again, Nora asked them if they would fulfill another fantasy of hers. They did, moving into a sixty-nine on the bed, cunt to mouth, pink flesh to pink tongues, while Nora sat and watched them in this, her favorite position. Inhibitions completely gone now, she even reached over and touched Robin's sweet ass with her own fingers. Unable to stop herself, spurred on by Robin's moans, she slipped her finger inside, amazed at the heat of this orifice, completely turned on by the fact that she was inside a woman being eaten by another. When they came, it was as if her own body was convulsing again, trembling with the heat of a climax.

After a long while, they slipped beneath the comforter, and Nora relaxed in their arms, warm under the duvet, held on both sides by women. Their skin was softer than she could imagine, and she loved the feeling of their nipples up against her, their flat bellies and their hairy mounds pressed tight against her.

And when Charlotte leaned over to brush her cunt, she responded in turn. Feeling another woman's pussy was no longer a fantasy, but the most natural thing in the world.

Chapter Six

Rachel

For some women, the act of dominating another is the central point of their sexuality. For me, it is important, but only a part of a whole complex lifestyle that I enjoy.

I begin with the clothing. I like to stand in front of

the mirror, but before I begin to dress, I look at myself. I am in love with my body. I love my hair, the way it falls into long dark waves that I can let hang loose when I want to be softly sensual, or put up into the most severe styles when I want to become an enforcer. I love my breasts, my flat stomach, the dark triangle between my legs that my submissives will do anything, even fight among themselves, to pleasure. A lot of people think narcissism is vain and unholy, but to me it is an essential part of the confidence that allows me to stand before another woman and order her to her knees.

I have a whole closet of clothing I have purchased specifically for domination, collected over the years from hundreds of places in dozens of cities. I literally have a suit of clothes for every mood I can find myself in. I have leather suits that cover me from my throat to my ankles, and devices made of straps and chains that cover nothing and are only worn to accentuate my naked body. I have rubber suits, clothing made of satin and lace, outfits in every color of the rainbow. If you're going to do something, you should do it right.

This morning I select a white lace corset, white stockings with lace tops, devilishly high white leather shoes. I've always been partial to this outfit because it looks so sweet, almost kind and virginal. It confuses the submissives because they don't expect someone wearing such clothing to be cold and cruel. I like to stay one step ahead of them always.

The one I am working with today is Marcia, a young woman I met through a fellow dominatrix. She told me about this submissive of hers and offered to loan her to me as a treat. I accepted immediately and ordered her to come to my house last night. As I dress, I realize that she has been downstairs all night, chained to a ring on the wall, lying on the cold hardwood floor.

She is awake when I walk into the room, and by her appearance she has been that way all night. I simply adore the way a leather collar looks when it is securely buckled about the neck of a submissive, especially one with a long, thin neck such as this one. She is small, well formed, curled up on the floor, and obviously very stiff.

I unsnap the chain from the ring set into the wall. It never fails to amaze me that they obtain such gratification from obeying my commands implicitly, for at any time she could have easily removed the chain herself, or even unbuckled the collar and taken it away from her throat. These lowly submissives are so drawn into their world of servitude and algolagnia that I have often detained them simply by ordering them to stay in one place. They have held so stlll, sometimes for several hours at a time, that had I used physical restraints it would have been only for their appearance.

I order this young slave to her feet. Last night, when she arrived, my only words to her were commands to undress, to lean forward into the collar, and to remain on the floor chained to the wall. She hardly knows me, has no idea what to expect. She is quick to obey, which pleases me, but her cramped muscles will not respond when she tries to stand. The white suit has done its job well, for I can see in her eyes that she thinks I will be lenient with her. When I am cruel and kick her with the sharply pointed toe of my shoe, only a small portion of her expression is related to pain; most of it is shock and surprise. She did not expect it, and now she has no idea what sort of treatment I have in mind for her. She struggles until she manages to get to her feet, somewhat shaky.

She knows the general atmosphere of the scene very well. She avoids my glance, looks mostly at the floor, refers to me as "Mistress," and does not speak unless spoken to. That part is easy for her: I have never met a dominatrix who did not insist on all of these things. What is more difficult for her is the knowledge that beyond the fundamental rules of behavior, we all have different preferences. It takes a long time for a submissive to know what pleases her Mistress, and even then, the rules can change with no warning, only consequences.

I look her over completely, deciding that her sweet little ass interests me the most. I order her to the floor again, this time on her hands and knees, and slowly I run my palm over the firm, pale cheeks. She holds her breath, her eyes closed, but right now I am as gentle as a lover with her. I can see her pussy starting to glisten with the dew that escapes from it, and I know that her clit must be throbbing with anticipation. Such a shame that she will not be given a chance to relieve it!

My pussy is stirring as well, but unlike this poor slut kneeling on the floor, I will have a chance to enjoy an orgasm, undoubtedly at her expense. If I had to analyze why I feel such a need to dominate these women,

I would find it difficult to fully explain, but the fact that I can demand sexual satisfaction at any time and receive it from someone who aches to give it to me is definitely one reason. I, of course, never have to consider giving it in return, for reciprocity is unheard of here.

Using the chain as a leash, I walk my captive to a chair on the far side of the room. The hardwood floor must be very painful on her knees, but she does not show her discomfort, and I am impressed. I frequently like to push my submissives to their limits, but I do not like whiners who cannot take even the lightest punishments. I think this one will be the treat I was promised.

I play with her a little. I slow right down, and she does as well, to stay in the proper position, as a dog might, at my heels. Then I take a few faster steps, and she falls behind, which gives me an opportunity to haul her along using the chain. Why do I love tormenting them so much? I do not know, but the sight of my hands on that leash, hauling this beautiful woman on her knees, warms my crotch immeasurably.

That ass is just too much for me to take; it looks too fresh, too pale, too untouched. I have an almost overwhelming desire to do something about it, and I sit down in the chair and haul her up by the chain, so that she is laid across my lap, helpless. She is trembling slightly, but I know by her wet pussy that there's more to it than just fear. She wants me to spank her just as much as I want to perform the deed. Knowing this, I caress her buttocks slowly and gently. It would be senseless to give her what she wants right away. It's a tease for both of us, and for her it's also torture, for she doesn't know how long I will be nice to her. For all she knows, I might not spank her at all. In a twisted, ironic way, that would be a nasty punishment all on its own.

Of course, I would not bring myself to this point without some satisfaction of my own. I choose my spot carefully, on the delicious curve of her left asscheek, and I bring my hand down as hard as I can.

Smack! I can feel the blow right through my arm, and by Marcia's gasp I know it hurts. I watch her ass intently, for here is my trophy. Right after the strike, her ass goes deathly white; seconds later, it comes up red, so that I can almost see the imprint of my palm.

I spank her again, on her right asscheek. Again it goes white and then comes up delightfully mottled with scarlet. She seems determined not to cry out, but I can feel her trembling. I know I must make her cry; it is my goal now.

I spank her again and again, first one asscheek, then another, then across both of them with my hand opened wide. She bites her lip and moans very softly. My pussy is aching now and I can imagine how my clit looks, large, peeking through the folds of my cuntlips, pink and firm. I can see hers; it is shiny and her pussylips are soaked.

Her face is red, both from the spanking and from her position, almost as red as her cute little ass. But she does not cry, only whimpers slightly when the blows strike her. I want to do more to her than just this, and I push her roughly to the floor. She looks at me with confusion, but she does not speak to me, and when I meet her eyes she quickly glances away, for it is not proper that she stare. I like that; someone has trained her well.

When I come back, I make sure she sees the leather paddle I have in my hand. I crack it twice across my own palm, and even though I use only a fraction of the force I will expend on her, it stings heartily on my hand. I can see the fear in her eyes now, and it warms me throughout and makes my cunt quiver with anticipation.

I do not speak any commands to her, but grab her by the collar and pull her to her knees. I force her to lie over the seat of the chair, with that tight red ass exposed to me. Her tits hang over the edge and I cannot resist reaching under her and twisting them hard. She moans and almost imperceptibly rubs her thighs together.

I put the paddle in front of her face and order her to kiss it. She does, almost lovingly, for I know that she both fears and respects this cruel device. Then I move back to her buttocks and raise the paddle high.

Thwack! Is there any sweeter sound than a leather paddle on submissive skin? She stiffens immediately and then, a moment later, goes completely limp.

The spot I struck was mottled red before, but now it is a brilliant scarlet, and it almost seems that I can see the pain welling up under the skin. The mark is square at the bottom, gently rounded at the top to match the outline of the paddle's leather face, and the welt rises noticeably. There *is* a reason why this is one of my favorite toys!

I batter her poor little ass unmercifully, until all of it

is burning red, from the small of her back to the tops of her legs. I'm so horny now I feel like I'm in heat. Her eyes are still tightly closed, and she whimpers almost continually, breathing hard through her mouth.

Then the first sob breaks, and then another, and the huge tears roll down her cheeks. "Please, Mistress, mercy!" she cries. I have won.

I am triumphant and we both know it well, but I still smack her hard twice more, one blow on each cheek, for she must not think that her request for mercy was granted. She is crying loudly now, and when I brush her vulva with the handle of the paddle her whole body jerks. I can imagine the pressure that has built up in that darling little pussy, and I smile because I know how uncomfortable it will be for her when it is not relieved.

I want relief as well, but unlike this poor creature, I can demand it. I toss her from the chair, and when she lands on the floor she moans as her injured butt connects with it.

I take off my panties and sit on the chair, my legs wide. "Pleasure me, slave," I order.

The expression on her face is now one of gratitude, and she is sincere when she whispers, "Thank you, Mistress, thank you!" She wastes no time in getting to her knees and putting her head between my thighs.

She is there for my use, and I take advantage of her. When I want her to lick a particular spot, I do not move my hips to accommodate her, but rather, I hold her head and position her so that her tongue reaches the place I want her to concentrate on. When I want her to speed up or slow down, I coldly give her an order and she obeys instantly.

I can see that she is holding her ass up, so that it does not touch her heels. Whenever I want a little extra thrill I push down hard on her shoulders, so that those bruised cheeks press against her feet. I am rewarded by the shudder that goes through her and the little whimper.

Her tongue slips effortlessly into the groove of my cunt, and I position her so that she licks me up and down on both sides of my hole before I have her concentrate there. She knows how to slip her tongue inside me, and I enjoy the feeling of heat and warmth at the entrance. I fuck myself with her tongue, pushing her into me and then pulling her back, and I can see my juice on her lips and face. I know that she would like to lick it off and drink it in, but I have not given her permission to do so.

I pull her by her long hair and move her up to the top of my slit, where my clit rests, waiting for a touch. A hot rush goes right through me when her tongue reaches it, but I am careful that she does not realize it. If she knew the pleasure she was giving me, she might be proud of it, and pride is something I will not tolerate in a submissive—save for the pride she may feel when she tells others that she is allowed to serve me.

I keep her there, on that swollen button, and she licks it relentlessly. I move one hand to reach down and grab her nipple, and I pinch it hard as she does. Her eyes are squeezed tightly again because of it, and together we continue, she in agony and I in ecstasy.

The fine line is crossed again and again, as her torture thrills her and excites me, and my pleasure becomes her pain.

All of my senses are now concentrated in that triangle between my legs, and I know that I will come soon. I think she can feel it as well, because she steps up her efforts even more. Her tongue is flying on my cunt. I feel a warmth that starts there and moves out all through my body, a tingling sensation that goes right to my spine. I hold my breath as it washes over me, and when it is finished, I immediately push her roughly away onto the floor.

She knows that she has made me come, but she will have no idea of the intensity, even though I am warmed right through and my whole body feels refreshed and light. Her mouth is soaked and I grant her the right to lick off my juice. Her enjoyment is sincere and I can see her savoring it as I might a fine wine.

That reminds me of lunch, and when I look at my watch I notice that I have only an hour before my date with Charlotte and Robin. I look at the young woman sprawled on the floor; she is still in the same position as when I threw her down. I am pleased by that. I do not like submissives who do anything without permission.

"I am going out," I say to her. "You will remain here, exactly as you are, until I return. Do you understand?"

"Yes, Mistress," she whispers, and I notice the light in her eyes. She is intelligent, she is respectful, but above all, she is obedient, and I have no doubt that she will not move while I am gone.

I leave then and go to my room to change my clothes.

Just before I go out, I check on my captive, and see to my satisfaction that she has not moved. At the last moment, I drop a pinch of food into my aquarium and watch as the colorful fish rise to the surface to eat. Normally they don't get fed until four, but I don't expect to be home until well after midnight.

Chapter Seven

Carly

When the room is dark and close like this, I can almost hear them all breathing. Some of them I can definitely hear, swift and easy in their throats, and these are the ones I will want first of all. When I can hear the breath, I can hear all of the warmth inside of them. The heat will melt my tongue and hold it in them all night.

Someone has to start them up, but tonight it will not be me; it was my privilege last week. Like a secret society we meet in this quiet room.

We hold the common thread of the arts and we are painters, composers, filmmakers, but to discourage the uninitiated we call this event "performance art" and issue only very special invitations.

I do not even remember who issued my invitation, or how long ago it was, but I remember my first time. I had heard that such societies existed but I had never thought I would see one, and yet there I was thrust into a room of dykes as outrageous as me with no rules to bind them. Now I am firmly entrenched and will not miss a meeting. Sometimes I even issue invitations of my own, and those so honored have never been disappointed.

The women sit around and they talk quietly. Sometimes I listen to their conversations and at other times I just sit and drink them in with all my senses. A few of them are fully dressed, a few are completely naked, and some wear costumes. One is pierced in so many places that when she moves she shimmers under the low lights, gold and harsh stainless steel rings and balls embedded in sweet, soft, dark skin. Did the needle sing for joy when it was thrust into that flesh? Surely the metal rings sighed when they closed around it. The needles have pierced my nipples also, and at the sight of her I touch the rings through my own tits. My nipples wept for a long time after and turned red as if branded. But now the gold is part of me, and I wear it proudly. I use it to invite the converts, and thrust it defiantly at the uninitiated.

I can see her looking at the jewelry embedded in me. She is eyeing the tattoo I have above my right ring and I wonder if that is her attraction: the waxing moon and the morning star seared there, colors of heat and calla lilies, Aurora rising from the shadows of the night. I did it mostly to feel the sensation of the ink burned in like fluid fire. Then I notice there is one beside her whose body is almost enveloped completely by the designs, yet she ignores her, and I know then that it is the rings she wants.

I meet her eyes across the room. They are green, deep, needful. Her lips open so slightly and they are wet. When she spreads her legs, I see that her mouth is not the only set of lips that are dampened. I catch my breath. She is closely shaved, completely bare. Pierced through the mons veneris is the tiniest circlet of gold (are they not wonderful words, the labia majora, the labia minora, the pudendum, the clitoris!). It pierces one side and then the other, and spans the space between them. I want that ring between my teeth. I know that I must have her.

I wait. I do not know who began the custom that a single person, preselected, must decide the moment that the meeting comes to order. This week it is the woman with the tattoos. I watch her. She is looking about the room slowly, decisively, making her selection, but I do not meet her eyes. I want to begin with that gold ring. I want to try to suck it right out of that skin.

The tattooed woman looks at me, looks past me. There is a woman on the floor in front of me. She is Japanese, almond-eyed, skin that seems like heavy honey has been spread evenly over it and left to soak in. I want to taste its sweetness later. It is she who the tattooed one chooses. When the tattooed woman crosses the room, she kneels before the Japanese woman. She is as gentle as a dream when she looks into her eyes and whispers the words to her. Then she grabs her, pulls her to her, roughly pushes the kiss into her. The Japanese woman responds in kind. The meeting has begun.

I nod to the pierced woman and she nods her assent, feverishly. We touch halfway across the room and she sinks to the floor under me. I hold her in my arms all the way down.

"The cunt ring," I tell her. "I have to have it."

"Take it, it is yours." she tells me. The room is no longer quiet but filled with voices, some low, some very loud. We are not cruel but we are rough and the words move through the air with a life of their own.

Fuck me, dyke. Stick your hand up there. Don't be so shy, I'm not going to fuckin' break. Ram that in, bitch.

She is under me and I am going to cover her completely right now to keep everyone else away. I am greedy and I am going to keep her for myself. My hands are on the nipple rings. She has a ring in her navel, a dozen in her ears. I am saving the cunt ring for last.

I kiss her and push my tongue into her. Her mouth

is hot and sweaty. Then she touches me and I almost come right there. She's got a pin through her tongue. I pull back and she sticks it out at me. There is a gold ball on top of it. I laugh and grip her tighter. When I kiss her again, I suck her tongue hard into my mouth. I want to swallow that ball, want to feel it go right through my body and come out like a ben-wah ball pushed in and out for my pleasure. It burns my tongue with the heat of her mouth.

I suck the taste of her off all the metal on her body. Her fingers are on the rings in my tits. My mouth is on her ears, my lips are in the curve below each breast, my tongue is in her navel, and it feels as deep and sweet as a tiny cunt. If I had a prick I would screw her there.

The ring below is permeated with the liquid of her cunt. I suck it until only the rich taste of the gold remains. I stick a fingernail into the circle, pull it from side to side. Her lips follow it in each direction. She moans each time.

"Pull it harder." I do. The lips stretch against it and it holds firm as the flesh yields to it. My other finger fits into the tip of her vulva. The fluid collects under my fingernail and I put it in her mouth. She drinks it greedily, like wine.

More. It isn't there to collect dust. Make it work for you. There is not a hair anywhere. She is sleek as stonewashed silk. The razor must hold its edges in when it passes over that flesh, afraid to leave the smallest mark in its wake. The cold steel meets the hot gold at the apex of that deep cavern and skirts it on all sides until the skin is bare. I would love to kiss it then and taste the tang of the shaving cream. The skin would be ruffled. I would have to lick it and make it lie smooth again.

I lick it now. The ring is a perfect circle between my lips and I capture my tongue in it. The sigh from her lips is the sound of sparkling wine as it rushes into the glass. I hear it there, but I taste it here.

The ring should melt from the heat here. I swirl my tongue into that flower and pull the nectar out from its depths.

"Fuck me!" I put my finger at the edge of the tunnel and push it in. She swallows it whole but it is not enough to satisfy her.

"Give me more. Give it to me hard, Carly, I want to be well and truly fucked."

I want to put my whole body in there. Two fingers, three, and they are held together with the sticky thick gum of her passion. I pull them out and suck them greedily. Just as greedily she begs me to put them back in. I push in all four fingers this time. They slide in as if they were greased. They go in as far as my knuckle.

My thumb takes her asshole. Give me all of it! There is a ring there too, a circle of muscle that holds me as firmly as I hold her. There is a special passion in being allowed into this most forbidden area.

A thin wall separates my thumb and my fingers and I can feel them moving deep in her cunt. The walls are slippery, ferociously hot, sweet as cider. I would like to stand alongside them, reach over my head, trapped inside of her, and caress them with my hands.

There is a touch on my legs. The woman is on her

hands and knees, coming over toward me. She does not say a word as she spreads my thighs. Her burgundy tongue snakes out to taste me, but once she has made contact, she eats me immediately, munches on me, sucks and blows her hot breath into my cavern. I can feel her tongue inside of me. It pushes right through my whole body and doesn't stop until it reaches into my fingers. Her tongue is deep enough to become part of my hand. She is eating the woman I am fucking with my fingers.

"Come to me, dyke," says the one I have impaled on my knuckles. My pleasure-giver moves her sweet ass on the carpet and I grab at the cheeks with my free hand. She is a big woman and my fingers sink deliciously into her. She is feathery, fluffy; I would like to pillow my head on her ass and feel her body surround me. When the mouth joins her cunt, we are a circle ourselves on the floor. We are as deeply embedded in flesh as the rings in my tits.

These two make sounds in their throats, sighs, moans, whispers, but they are almost lost in the cadence that fills this close room. It is a symphony of woman voices. In the corner I can hear the smack of a hand spanking a naughty ass. Close by my ear I can hear cunts rubbing together. The wiry pubic hair crackles when it touches and pulls. I think I can hear my own voice when there is a lull.

This woman would suck out my flower and give it back to me on the tips of her fingers like a jewel. She is relentless but she matches my mood. I fuck with my fingers and she fucks me with her tongue. She looks familiar to me; I think that some weeks ago I spread her cunt with my fingers and pushed a dildo inside. I remember how her lips swelled around it and I know that mine are doing just this around her tongue. I have it tightly in the grip of my pussy and if I move she will have to follow me. I buck my hips to feel the touch of her on all of me. She follows me when I do.

There is no richer smell than that of pussy. This one is a thick perfume and I get close so I can take it in. I smell her ass too, my thumb still deep inside it, and find it as tantalizing. I stay there, breathing her in. She fills me just as I fill her, completely, drenchingly.

My hand is now wet to the wrist and I can feel her tightening around me. She is whimpering; she wants to cry to me and tell me to make her come, but she can't because her mouth is licking a clit. She gestures instead. She grabs my hand, slippery and hot, and pumps it into her holes. I am her dildo, going in and out for her. When she gives herself over to coming, it is long and luscious. She is so wet I could slip myself into her completely.

Someone else is here beside me; I can feel fingers on my back. The two lovers I am joined with become aware of her presence. We move as if following a script and it becomes a wicked dance. The neophyte lies on her back, offering herself up to me. When I take her I feel like I have slipped on top of a virgin. Beside me, the two I have left join together mouth to cunt. We lie parallel, two by two.

No razor has ever touched the ruby lips of this woman. She is hairy, more than I have ever seen, and I open my lips and take the tuft of hair into my mouth without touching her skin at all. She is a meadow, with drops of dew sparkling on the edges of the hair. I suck them off onto my tongue. Then I push the hair aside and reach the sweetmeat hidden by it. I can feel her whole body move each time I rub across her clitoris. She is a rare woman, one completely attuned to her sex. I want to hold her when she comes.

She is on me at the same moment and I chill right through to my skin. She can pull hot and cold out of me with the same breath. Her tits are mashed into my belly, so tender. With my hands I pull the nipples free and play with them. She copies my movements. Her fingertips are cool and refreshing on me.

"You are wetter than anyone I have had here."

"Drink it in, sweets, there's plenty more."

"Honey and milk are under thy tongue."

"I want to fuck you until I'm exhausted." For a little while there are other hands on us. A finger is thrust into my hole while my cunt is licked by the woman lying below me. Hands grasp my asscheeks and move me in rhythm to the tongue that thrills me. I cannot see who it is and this excites me more. I push into my lover's crack as hard as I can. She squeals and squirms on the floor. My skin tingles when she rubs against it. A hand explores the cunt I am licking and pushes the hair into my nose and chin. Then the hands are gone, and we are together again, alone with each other but bound to everyone in the room.

Another woman comes up to us and lies on the floor in front of us. Her face is near the pussy I am licking.

Our eyes meet and her intentions are clear. I move up to the clit, flicking my tongue over the top part. The woman slinks in and I can smell her perfume. She licks the lower part and together we pleasure every bit of that hairy treasure.

The woman is going wild beneath me. I hold her tightly now in my arms. My own pussy is throbbing with each touch of her tongue on me. She has her hands free, her fingers are moving, they probe into me and fill me. We are just cunts and tongues now.

She is hot, she is wet, and now she is coming. Both of us bear down on that soft rose and suck it out of her. She is a screamer. I hold her down and savor her convulsions beneath me with my mouth still on her crotch. She is moist all over. I would love to lick every inch of her.

When she is finished, my new companion beckons me to rise. I get to my knees slowly, so that my cunt is never without a tongue on it. I face this woman, redheaded and slender. She kneels over the hairy snatch we have just licked. She rubs her own wet slit on it and grabs my tits as she does. The gold rings flash as she tugs them gently. "Harder." My nipples are long and firm when she pulls them.

No one is forgotten here. The redheaded woman puts the fingers of one hand in her mouth. They emerge, slick and shiny from their cocoon. Her grin is that of an elf. She puts her hand behind her without looking, with her eyes on mine; we share a secret. Her clit is taking its pleasure from the pubic mound below her, but she is giving it back: The wetted fingers are probing. The mouth below me sighs. The redheaded woman winks at me. I lean forward and kiss her. I can't put my tongue deeply enough in her mouth. I wish it was long enough to reach right down her throat.

The tongue in me is longer than any I have felt. It curves around me and fills me. She is caressing my womb with it. It must be hot and close in there, the wellspring of the juices that flow down and cover her lips, her tongue, her chin.

There is a place that is the very center of me. All bones, all nerves, all muscles begin and end at it, and now her tongue has found it. She tweaks it, flicks across it, kisses it with her lips and nibbles at it with her teeth.

Right there, yes, right there. She licks it, eats it, gobbles it with a hunger. She is on both sides of it, now in the middle. Suck that clit, honey, make it come! It is a solid bar through the top of my cunt and I can feel it swollen and hard there. My whole crotch is swollen with sex, sex-filled lips, sex-filled vagina, sex is a flood that overflows through me and seeks to crash like a wave out of me through my snatch. When I come, it will escape and pour relentlessly over her. She will be soaked in my sex, she will drown in it, and I will kiss her and drink it back in.

My partner on top twists my ring with her fingers and for a moment there is a twinge of pain, but it only heightens my arousal. Then she grabs my tit and squeezes it firmly. The liquid sex held there rushes through me down to the fire between my legs, but instead of extinguishing it, it stokes it. I am heavy there and the pressure is throbbing. Surely she can feel it pulsating on her tongue. The sweet ache must be filling her mouth.

Then the floodgates open and I am swept along with the flow. I can hear myself scream from far away. It rushes in my ears and pushes me over the edge, but like the surf, the waves just keep coming as she continues to lick my cunt. My thighs are soaked with heat and wet. She cannot breathe, I am grinding so hard on her mouth. She wants to take all of me into her and I am willing to go.

There are hands all over me, urging me to lean back, and I do. I put myself into their grip and they lay me on the floor. I am told to close my eyes and I do. Now I am the center of their circle, and they come from all sides to please me. I do not know how many hands are there, how many cunts, how many mouths, but they are everywhere. There is a tongue pressing on my cunt and a finger in my ass. There are mouths on my tits, playing with the rings. There is a pussy on my mouth, and I gladly open myself and probe it with my tongue. It is hot and soaked, it has already come once, but I will make it come again. I can taste many women in it. Through one cunt I am licking them all.

My ears are filled with the sound of them, and it is obvious that pleasure is not mine alone. The ones on my nipples have fingers in their pussies. The woman licking my slit is having her own licked, and there is one behind her again. I am the cynosure and my waves radiate through them all. Even the ones on the outside of the circle can feel the heat of my cunt. There is too much for me alone; I have to share it with them.

The spasm catches me by surprise. I give it back through my mouth to the pussy I am licking, I give it through my nipples like milk to the ones sucking there. White hot, it sears through them and leaves them breathless. It leaves me panting and weak; I have given up all the force to them and my limbs are heavy and soft in its wake. My nerves have all moved to the edges of my skin and wait there to be stroked by the hands that caress me gently. At first I am too hot and raw to be touched, but then the hands are soothing, and I relax and try to breathe. They have taken me further than I thought I could ever go.

Two of them are lying with me now, whispering to me and stroking the length of my body. Their skin is cool next to mine and feather soft. I could lie forever in the protective circle of their arms and they know it.

They kiss me, lick my throat, cup my pussy with their hands, and hold the heat inside it.

Incredibly lousy prose, Carly.

Extraordinary sex, though, I say.

Chapter Eight

End of Season

The sun was just starting to go down and the sky was a brilliant crimson. Charlotte was relaxed, enjoying the drive, one hand on the wheel, while Robin looked all around with the excitement of a child at Christmas.

"I can hardly believe I'm finally going to get to see Provincetown," she said. "Do you know how many times I've said to myself that I have to visit? But every time the store always got too busy, or something else came up, and I just put it off."

"Well, I know you're going to be very pleased with it," Charlotte said. "I haven't been here in years, but I'm sure it hasn't changed too much, and Liz has one of the nicest cottages on the Cape."

They had the windows open, and the air that streamed in was cool. It was almost the end of the tourist season and mercifully, traffic on the small highway was sparse, although the crab shacks were doing a brisk business on this Friday night.

Their destination was indeed an exciting one. Provincetown, Massachusetts, a gay mecca perched on the edge of Cape Cod, quaint and touristy, quiet and exciting all at the same time. Many years ago, when Charlotte had visited, she had met Liz and subsequently spent the entire week with her. Since that time they had kept up a long-distance friendship. When Liz had invited the pair to spend a weekend at her home there, Charlotte told the agency she would be taking the Friday off, Robin entrusted the store to her assistant manager, and they threw their bags in the trunk and headed to the ocean.

"How much further?" Robin asked.

"You sound like my kid brother did when we went on trips," Charlotte teased. "Relax. It always seems to take forever on this highway, but once we get there it'll be worth it, you'll see."

She reached across the seat. Robin was wearing white shorts, and Charlotte stole a glance at the delightful way her chocolate skin contrasted with them. Her thighs were smooth, rich, and powerful, and Charlotte's fingers strayed up and down them. Robin slumped in the seat and opened her legs wider. Charlotte's fingers could feel the heat through the cotton.

"No underwear?" she smiled.

"You always complain when you've got to stop and take it off," Robin grinned. The shorts were fairly loose and it was easy for Charlotte to push the leg aside and gain access to the naked pussy under them. Robin sighed deeply and pulled the shorts away herself so that her dark hair peeked through them. She loved having Charlotte's fingers there, and when Charlotte found her clit, the black woman groaned out loud.

"You're pretty wet," Charlotte said, as she slipped her finger over and around the hard nub of pink flesh she had found. "When did all this happen?"

"I was thinking about you," Robin said, as she moved closer on the seat so Charlotte could finger her fully. "And these seats are pretty nice, you know. Really comfortable cushions. It's hard not to squirm on them every so often."

"Is that all you ever do, keep yourself turned on?" Charlotte teased, but she felt Robin's fingers on her own leg, reaching up the leg of her own shorts, and looking down she saw the dark skin of Robin's hand come away wet.

"Sure is," Robin smiled, "just the same as you do."

Unencumbered by driving, Robin could concentrate on what she was doing, and once she had slipped her finger into Charlotte's hole and noticed how loud the resulting moan was, she turned on the seat sideways and used one hand to push Charlotte's loose shorts aside while her other hand busied itself in the hot, moist folds there.

"People can see us," Charlotte protested.

"Honey, this is the biggest car on the road," Robin laughed. "Only a tractor-trailer could see in here. Besides, when did you ever care if anyone could see?"

"Point and match," Charlotte conceded, and then drew in her breath sharply as Robin's fingertip slid effortlessly into her soaked hole once again.

The scenery was forgotten as Robin leaned down on the seat to be closer to her prize. She was close enough to see the dark hairs peeking out through the leg of Charlotte's shorts, and when she breathed deeply she could smell the rich perfume that she loved so much. She pushed on Charlotte's thigh and watched appreciatively as Charlotte moved her left leg as far away as possible, exposing as much pussy as she could.

"I'm supposed to be driving," Charlotte protested faintly, even as she squirmed a little on the seat in response to the dark-skinned finger that was probing this most intimate and wet area.

"I can stop if you like," Robin threatened, smiling, and was not disappointed when Charlotte told her that she could carry on just as she was. So encouraged, she wiggled on the seat until she could get close enough to put her head in Charlotte's lap. Charlotte tilted the wheel up to accommodate her and gasped a moment later when she felt the whisper-soft tip of Robin's tongue and her hot breath brush achingly sweet on her clit.

It teased both of them because Robin could not gain access to all of Charlotte's pussy; Charlotte's shorts and the restrictions of the car meant that Robin could only reach a small area. It heightened her own pleasure when she was able to stretch out her tongue as far as she could and touch the heat of Charlotte's clit with it, and her fingers wove their way around the fabric to gain access to the slippery hole that she knew so well.

Charlotte was wearing a loose cotton shirt with no bra under it, and Robin was able to reach up under the tail of it and snake her hand to the tits she adored. Charlotte drew in her breath as the familiar fingers tweaked her nipples the way she liked. Robin couldn't fully reach her left one, but she was able to just brush against the rock-hard nub and feel its heat on the tips of her fingers. Then she put her hand back between Charlotte's legs and worked her clit over in earnest.

"You do know what I like," Charlotte whispered. She was paying special attention now to her driving, determined to function safely even as the burning thrills went through her. She shivered all over as Robin touched the very tip and pushed it back and forth. When she stopped for a red light, she breathed deeply, relaxed and gave herself over to the sensations. When the light turned green, it was difficult to concentrate again on what she was doing.

"That's the spot right there, isn't it?" Robin asked,

touching Charlotte with a wet fingertip. The sharp intake of breath told her that she had found her mark.

Of course, it was all part of the game, for she knew every inch, every spot, every sweet hair of her lover's pussy. She stayed there, looking up at Charlotte and enjoying the fact that she was causing so much pleasure. Charlotte's hands were firmly clenched on the wheel and she was trying to keep her breathing regular.

"Damn! Another green light," Charlotte murmured under her breath, and then she had to smile. If she was in a hurry they'd all be red. Now that she wanted to stop and enjoy the rush that was coursing through her, she was sure there would be nothing but green lights all the way to the tip of the Cape.

She looked in the rearview mirror; there was no traffic behind her. She slowed down, looking intently at the green light up ahead, trying to think about how slowly she should drive to reach it when it was red. It was hard to think when her whole body was focused on the soft wet folds between her legs where Robin's fingers caressed her clit so softly and lusciously. Turn red, turn red, turn red, she chanted to herself. I want to come.

In answer to her prayers, the light turned yellow for a maddeningly long time, and then to the much-anticipated red. She brought the big car to a stop, sighed, and once again let herself go. Robin knew that she was close and she stepped up her movements on the soaked flesh. Back and forth, up and down she pushed the turgid button, which was firm yet yielding under her fingers. Her hand and the leg of Charlotte's shorts were wet with highly perfumed liquid.

"Isn't this better than just driving?" Robin asked. She felt naughty doing this—hadn't she always been taught never to distract the driver?—and so carefree as she massaged Charlotte's clit. She knew just how the tingling sensation was going through Charlotte's body, and her own cunt was hot and wet as she made love to her lover.

"Right there—oh—oooh!" Charlotte threw her head back and relaxed completely, letting the ripples multiply and swell until her whole body was on fire. She almost cried out as the last waves went through her, and then she slumped in the seat, satisfied.

"Light's green, dear," Robin said matter-of-factly, as she sat up and played the sweet innocent. "Hey, a saltbox house! Check it out."

It was dusk when the highway brought them to the water's edge. Robin was fascinated with the beach, with the salt grass that grew up from the sand and the relentless movement of the water as it moved in to lap at the shore and then return to the sea, leaving foam and shells in its wake.

They drove into the town, but they were moving too quickly for Robin to drink everything in. This was the residential area, neat cottage-sized houses side-by-side with their wooden shingles and driveways finished in chalky white clamshells, their gardens tended with almost fanatical devotion. It was so completely different from the city that she felt she had found another world.

The cottage they ended up at was fairly large, actually an all-season house masquerading as a summer residence, finished in natural wood that had weathered to a delightful silver color. There was a porch containing comfortable, well-worn chairs that made Robin think of cool drinks on a hot summer night. They parked in the driveway and then went up to the front door. Only the screen was closed and Charlotte knocked on its wooden frame. A cheery, "Come in, it's open," greeted them and they went inside.

Much of the furniture was sturdy and summery, solid wood with overstuffed cushions finished in flowery cotton, braided rugs. Mixed in with this were a mirror with a wild brass frame, a table made of discarded car parts welded together, a planter frame handmade of twigs, an unusual painting on one wall, a light made of beaten brass with fascinating patterns. Somehow these wildly artistic pieces did not clash with the traditional furniture but complemented it in an offbeat way.

A woman came in from the back room. Robin took a long look, admiring what she saw. She was well built, her dark hair wavy to her shoulders, her breasts deliciously firm under her thin T-shirt. Her only makeup was bright pink lipstick which accentuated her infectious smile. Robin couldn't imagine her doing anything but smiling.

"Charlotte!" The exclamation was full of laughter and joy, and then she had her friend in a huge hug, swinging gently back and forth. She stopped, pulled away, looked her up and down, and then hugged again. When they finally parted, Charlotte had pink lipstick on her cheek and her lips.

"This is Robin," Charlotte began, but Liz didn't wait for formal introductions. She took the hand Robin offered, and then pulled her close and hugged her. Robin couldn't help but return it, at first shyly, then as confidently as the woman who was holding her. Liz's friendliness was a drug that intoxicated.

"Well, I'm not going to spend the whole night standing here," Liz said. "Your bags can stay right there. You come in here and sit down."

They did. Although it was a bit chilly outside, the room was warm and the cotton cushions felt soothing when they sat down. Robin was fascinated by the painting over the sofa, and she got up to look at it more closely.

It was painted in a faintly abstract style, but immediately recognizable as a woman. She was nude and dark-haired, and if the face was difficult to see clearly, the exaggerated pink nipples, hard and erect, were not. One hand was between the legs, caressing the dark triangle that was faintly visible between the fingers. The painting was as erotic and captivating as any photograph; the artist had expertly captured the thrill of self-loving in bold sweeps of color on the canvas.

"That's a wonderful picture, isn't it?" Liz said, as she saw Robin admiring it. "It was painted by a woman named Leslie Sullivan, a local artist. It was in the front window of the gallery down the street and I couldn't leave it there. I had to have it."

"It really is amazing," Charlotte said. "It's completely explicit and yet it doesn't really show anything."

"It was funny to stand and watch people on the street," Liz laughed. "They'd walk by it and look at it quickly, and then they'd stop and look at it again. You could tell that a lot of people were getting turned on just standing on the sidewalk and looking at it."

"So you bought it," Robin mused.

"I had to," Liz said. "We have a neighborhood prude here—I really can't understand why she stays here, because she's just disgusted by the fact that we're all so liberal in this town. Every week she's got a letter in the paper saying we're all going to rot in hell; I think the editor just prints them for their amusement value.

"Anyway, she has to walk past this gallery every day to go to work, and every day she'd stop and look at it, with this really sour look on her face. She would just stand there and whenever anyone walked by, she'd stop them and carry on about how sinful the picture was. What was so funny was that it was obvious she was being turned on by the picture—everyone could see that!—but she had her reputation to maintain and so she'd stand there and screw up her face while she was getting all wet. I had to buy it. I figured if it stayed there much longer she'd go raving insane."

"It looks just great there," Charlotte said. "I should get something like that to put in our living room."

"It was the only place I could put it," Liz said. "If I hung it in my bedroom I'd wake up every morning and be so turned on I'd spend all my time with my hand in my cunt, and I'd be late for work."

Robin was at first shocked that Liz was so graphic in front of someone she'd only just met. That only lasted for a moment, though, and quickly turned to intrigue as a thought entered her mind. The possibility had only crossed her mind once or twice before, but now that she'd met this captivating woman.... She put the thought out of her mind, though, when her pussy started to throb. There would be plenty of time for that later.

Liz, it turned out, was a writer who lived year-round in Provincetown. Several days each week she worked at a local newspaper—"I started out as their restaurant reviewer," she said, "but in a town this small, I had to branch out pretty quickly!"—and the rest of the time she turned out articles and novels from an airy, window-lined office in the back of the house.

"What kind of subjects?" Robin asked.

"Just about anything," Liz replied. "I like to write what I call 'beach books,' light reading that people take with them on vacation. But my favorite is erotic. I like to write books about sex."

Robin was even more intrigued after that, and each time she looked at Liz, she noticed something new: the way her thighs looked so creamy at the line of her shorts, the depression where her throat met her chest, so ripe for a tongue to tickle, her long fingers and her slim ankles, one decorated with a tattoo of two cherries on a stem. At times she woke herself with a start, when the conversation turned to a hum in her head and she realized that she was deep in thought, imagining sex with Charlotte, sex with Liz. To her, the whole room, dominated by the woman with her hand between her legs, was thick with the syrup of sex.

"You've never been to Provincetown, have you, Robin?" Liz asked, and when the black woman shook her head, she got up and said, "Well, it sure is nice this time of day."

It would get cool at night, she warned them, and so the two travelers took their bags to the guest room to change. Robin stopped and looked around from the doorway. Not only was it a spare bedroom but it was also the overflow for Liz's thousands of books. Shelves lined the walls, and she had to stop herself before she got too caught up at looking at them all.

One shelf was very unusual, for although it contained several titles, all of them were duplicated four or five times. "Those are some of the books Liz wrote," Charlotte explained, and Robin tilted a few of them back to see the covers. There were four author names, a pseudonym for each variety of book. One name was devoted to the light reading that Liz had called "beach books"; another was for a cookbook series including a book on wine. Two of them were more to Robin's taste, though, for the covers and the titles suggested some pretty hot chapters inside. She would definitely return to these later.

The walk into town was both pleasant and fascinating. The business section, while fairly busy with cars, was designed for pedestrians, and Robin couldn't believe her eyes when she saw women walking arm-in-arm with women, men holding hands with men, same-sex couples sharing kisses on the street completely unconcerned. She had heard it was like this, but it was still a surprise when it really was true.

The three women went into a bar for a drink. The quiet lounge was softly lit and she could see couples sharing touches under the tables or kisses at the bar stools. She felt an almost overwhelming urge to kiss

Charlotte deeply right there, and when Liz got up to go to the washroom, she did. It was exciting and intoxicating to share such a forbidden kiss and her pussy throbbed so much she had to squirm on her chair for a bit of relief. She wished she could touch herself there and rub the hot nectar between her fingertips. Charlotte was just as turned on and returned the kiss with heated passion.

"You don't have to be embarrassed to do anything in front of Liz," Charlotte told her. "I know you're shy, having just met her, but you'll see. She's cool about everything."

"Maybe in time," Robin said.

"I know you well enough," Charlotte smiled. "I don't think it will take long at all."

When Liz came back, they finished their drinks and decided to resume their walk. By this time it was getting late and the sidewalks were becoming empty. Charlotte yawned and apologized, citing the long drive that they'd made that day.

"That was pretty rude of me," Liz said. "I never thought about you being tired. Let's go back home." Robin desperately wanted to see more of this fascinating town, but when she thought about the alternative, she firmly decided that sightseeing could wait. Right now all she wanted was to feel Charlotte's warm body beside her in bed.

They walked back along the residential streets. Despite the cool air, a number of people were sitting on their porches enjoying the end of the season, and a few of them called a greeting to Liz as the threesome walked by. Some were women with women, some men with women, some men with men, and Robin was taken with the heady sensual atmosphere and the carefree attitude that seemed to envelope the whole town. She could be happy here, she decided.

They got back to Liz's house, where their hostess made them a pot of tea, which they enjoyed in the living room. Robin's eyes kept straying to the painting and the more she looked, the more maddening it became; she wanted to cross the room and take Charlotte right there, wanted to pull at her clothes until the skin was bare and the hot wet pussy open for her to have. Of course Charlotte and Liz had much to catch up on, but Robin noticed that Charlotte's eyes kept straying to the abstract-faced woman with her hand between her legs, and it seemed that after she had glanced at it a few times, she made an effort to drain her cup quickly and mention that she was tired, too.

Liz kissed both of them good-night, and Robin found herself returning the kiss happily, although not as long or as deeply as she would have liked. Then the couple were in the book-lined bedroom, and Robin stared admiringly as Charlotte neatly folded her clothes and stood naked before her.

"I think we should do some reading before bedtime," Charlotte said. Robin's heart sank. "Reading?" she said. "I've been horny all night and now you want to sit up and read?"

Her expression changed immediately, though, when she saw that Charlotte had paused in front of the shelf that held Liz's books. After some consideration, she chose one of the erotic novels and lay on the bed, leafing through it.

Hot with anticipation, Robin took off her own clothes and put them on the back of a chair. Charlotte looked over and drank in the sight. No matter how many times she had seen Robin nude, she was still transfixed. The skin was like melted chocolate, the breasts were sweet orbs heavy with desire. The triangle of hair between Robin's legs was thick and short and it accented more than hid anything. Her legs were long and well formed, her belly flat and inviting, her feet small and delicious. Charlotte finally had to tear herself away and turn her attention back to the page she had opened to. It did not take long to find the passage she was seeking.

"'She ran her hands under my tits and pushed them together, then sucked my nipples into her mouth and licked the tips of them,'" Charlotte read. She looked over at Robin, who was unbuttoning her blouse. "'She rubbed her own nipples over them, through her clothes. She tickled them with her hair, and blew gently on them to cool them off. Then she took them into her warm mouth. That made me groan with pleasure.'"

As Charlotte continued reading, Robin bent over her and took both creamy white breasts between her dark fingers. Charlotte paused just a moment, with a whisper of a sigh, and then read some more. She paused again when Robin's warm lips brushed her breasts and the tip of her tongue snaked out to circle each nipple with exquisite warmth and softness. Her breasts were always sensitive, but tonight after their walk and the painting, they were bundles of sensual nerves just aching to be touched.

"Read it out loud to me," Robin begged, as she bent over her lover and sucked hungrily on her tits. This was a game they had never played before, but she loved hearing the words spoken in Charlotte's voice.

"'Again she used her tongue to draw long strokes on my body, from my breasts down to my belly. I was getting hotter and hotter as she moved closer to my soaked pussy.'"

Robin used the book as her coach, licking the smooth white skin between Charlotte's breasts and moving down her belly, lapping with her tongue wide. Charlotte's skin was slightly salty and she savored the taste of it as she went. When she got to the dark triangle of hair she stopped; the book had not gone that far yet. She busied herself licking the hairline and blowing on the cleft that started at the very top of Charlotte's warm, wet cunt, waiting to hear more.

"'Her first flick across my clit made me gasp,'" Charlotte continued. Her voice was whispery now, and Robin knew that was a sure sign that her tongue was doing its job very well. "'She licked me slowly the whole length of my pussy. I shivered and moaned as she stroked my clit with just the tip of her tongue.'"

For the second time that day, Robin caught the taste of Charlotte's delicious pussy in her mouth. As the book had described, she touched the tip of the clit with the tip of her tongue, the tiniest proportion of flesh to flesh. She had planned to keep doing that, but it was too much for her to resist, and after just a moment she was licking in earnest. The salty sweet taste flooded her mouth and she wanted to drink all of it in. If Charlotte had filled her completely, she would still have begged for more.

With signals and gentle touches, as familiar for both of them as words, Charlotte had Robin turn around on the bed and place herself on top. This was her favorite position, and she moaned at the touch of Robin's tongue on her pussy before she applied herself to the ruby-rich folds that were positioned so invitingly over her mouth. Robin gasped. She had been waiting so long that the pent-up emotions almost overcame her at that very first touch.

They were moaning so loudly that Robin was sure Liz would be able to hear them, but she didn't care at that point. All that mattered was the cunt below her and the tongue in her own pussy. She wet one finger and slipped it easily into Charlotte's tunnel. Charlotte, in turn, soaked her finger in the pussyjuice that shone on Robin's cunt and then eased it gently into the tight hole between Robin's smooth buttocks. Robin gasped at the completely full feeling and licked even harder and faster in her passion.

At a touch from her lover, Robin rolled over, and now both were on their sides. Pulling back a little, Charlotte could now move her free hand and reach the dark orbs that she loved to touch so much. The nipples were firm and ripe for squeezing, hot under her fingertips. Robin groaned, her mouth filled with Charlotte's cunt, her ass filled with Charlotte's finger. She was completely lost in all of it and could see nothing, hear nothing, taste nothing but the waves of sex that coursed through her.

Charlotte, likewise, was completely taken with what she was doing. When the heat in her pussy got too close to the bursting point she would concentrate more on Robin's pussy until she had calmed down a little. It was too soon to come just yet, and she wanted to make it last as long as she possibly could. When Robin pulled her cunt back a bit, Charlotte knew why. Both of them were more interested in building up right now, for each touch of tongue, each thrust of finger was too exquisite to stop. They could go at each other all night like this.

They knew each other so well that it became a game for both of them. When one would move slightly, to hold off, the other would increase whatever she was doing. Charlotte wiggled her finger inside Robin's ass, marveling at the intense heat and how the thickly muscled walls resisted her movements yet were so sweetly elastic at the same time. Then she pulled her finger out, almost all the way, until only the very tip was still inside, about to slip out beyond the boundaries of the muscular ring at the entrance. Robin sighed, but then groaned out loud when Charlotte pushed her finger back in, gently but firmly, in one fluid motion until it was in right up to her knuckle. Robin responded by fucking Charlotte's hole with two of her fingers, inserted and then slightly spread to contact all of this sweetest entrance into her lover's body. Now both of them were determined, for each wanted to be the one to give an orgasm first.

Charlotte won. Robin was just too excited, and had been so horny all evening, that she finally gave up her resolve and let herself drift with the tide that started between her legs and moved right through her entire body. She squirmed hard on Charlotte's mouth, grinding herself in, wishing that Charlotte's fingers could reach right up into the heat of her ass. When she finally stopped trembling, she was covered with sweat, breathing hard, but she never took her mouth off Charlotte's pussy.

Now that she had won, Charlotte gave herself up as well and let Robin's tongue work its magic on the most sensitive places between the folds of her cunt. When she came she almost cried out, and so Liz wouldn't hear, she bit her lip and gasped, long rasping breaths, until the final shivers were finished.

They snuggled together under the covers the book forgotten and fallen on the floor. Charlotte was completely relaxed, with Robin's head on her shoulder, and she sank into the pillow, looking around the room and reading the spines of the books in the shelf next to her.

She turned to talk to Robin when a title caught her eye, but found her lover fast asleep on her shoulder. Gently she kissed her forehead and turned out the light.

They both woke to the light streaming through the window, and although Robin was shy, Charlotte insisted that her heavy bathrobe was sufficient. Indeed it turned out to be, for Liz was in a spotless white terrycloth one, making coffee in the small, cozy kitchen.

She kissed them both before she poured coffee for them. This was taken in the back room, a large, airy sunporch screened in with the winter storm windows removed. There was still a touch of the evening chill in the air, but the sun streaming through was erasing the last of it. Both Robin and Charlotte sighed with delight when they sank into the overstuffed chairs and sipped their coffee. They were always so busy at their jobs that it was only when they took time to relax that they realized just how stressed they were.

"Today I'd like to take you back into town and let you walk through it," Liz said, as she also sat down with her coffee. "It's really nice early in the morning. And in the afternoon, you should go down to see the sand dunes."

"Well, it was nice of you to invite me here," Robin said.

Liz smiled. "As they say, any friend of Charlotte is a friend of mine."

Robin took another sip of her coffee. She wondered just what kind of relationship Charlotte and Liz had actually shared back then. Strangely enough, she felt no jealousy sitting in the room with a woman who might have been her partner's lover. It had been long before she had met the tall, dark-haired beauty, and she was not concerned. Instead, she found herself drawn to the ebullient, pink-lipsticked woman as much as she knew Charlotte must be.

She was even more intrigued when Liz got up to refresh their coffee cups. Her white terry robe was only very loosely tied, and when she bent down to pour the hot liquid, the robe separated and Robin was treated to the sight of Liz's large, delightful globes. The nipples were huge, larger than any Robin had seen before, and she could almost feel her mouth watering at the sight of them.

"Liz, you're flashing us," Charlotte said, but it was more a lighthearted comment than an admonition.

To Robin's surprise, their hostess was not the least embarrassed and she made absolutely no effort to correct the situation. "We're all women here," she said, and then she moved over to fill Robin's cup. When she did that, the ties gave way completely, and the robe swung open to show off her lovely body. Robin could not even think about her manners; she just stared.

"You are a shameless hussy," Charlotte teased.

"Oh, have a little mercy," Liz laughed. "I was lying in bed listening to you two going at it and I was horny all night. I can't believe I waited this long."

"Then wait no longer," Charlotte said, and she put down her coffee cup, stood up, took Liz into her arms, and kissed her hard.

Robin's mouth dropped open and she almost spilled her coffee, but she regained her composure almost immediately when Charlotte reached for her hand and pulled her to her feet. Threesomes were far from unusual for the pair and when Robin felt Liz's warm lips on her own, it was as natural as breathing. She returned the kiss with a passion that rose within her and spilled over to all three of them.

Without a word they walked together into Liz's bedroom. It was a fairly large room and the huge windows poured sunlight onto the white linen on the bed. They dropped their robes onto the floor and Liz openly admired Robin's dark-skinned body before dropping to her knees in front of her.

Robin grasped her intentions immediately, and she stood close and opened her legs. She was rewarded with the heat of Liz's tongue on the cleft of her pussy. Charlotte, meanwhile, stood behind Robin, put her arms around her, and held her breasts, playing with the nipples that were now hard and engorged.

Liz was very good at what she was doing. She rimmed all around Robin's hole and then pushed her tongue into it. At the same time, Charlotte moved one hand down and expertly slipped a finger into Robin's other hot hole. Robin groaned, twice filled.

"Now you know why I'm so fond of dark meat," Charlotte said, as she rubbed her tits against Robin's smooth back.

"Absolutely delicious," Liz said, pausing just long enough to speak before plunging her tongue back between Robin's legs.

"Hey, don't be greedy!" Robin joked, even as she gasped at the intensity of Liz's mouth on her pussy. "Some of us like white meat, especially if it's one we've never tried before."

The heat on her cunt was exquisite, but Robin's fingers were itching to touch those huge nubs on Liz's tits. She couldn't reach them and she begged to be able to put her hands on them. Liz smiled and licked some more; she knew that she had the upper hand here, for as much as Robin wanted those nipples, she also wanted Liz to keep munching on her pussy as long as possible. Liz loved it. She could tease and satisfy simultaneously.

Meanwhile, Charlotte knelt down on the floor as well, behind Robin. With a hand stroking one buttock, she licked the other one in long laps. Her tongue slid smoothly over the gentle curve of Robin's ass, leaving shiny wet streaks on the skin. Then she poked her tongue into the crack of Robin's ass and slid along it. The cheeks on either side of her tongue were deliciously warm, and when she got to Robin's tightly puckered asshole, she teased it with the very tip of her tongue. Robin groaned loudly and thrust her ass backwards to get even more of this lovely treatment. Charlotte gave her exactly what she wanted, pushing her tongue as far as she could into the recesses of this most forbidden entrance. Liz, who knew exactly what Charlotte was doing, pushed her tongue into Robin's wetness. It felt like Robin was trying to pull it deep into herself.

Robin could easily imagine having both of them enveloped in her body. The heat and wetness made her feel like her whole lower body was liquid, and it was difficult to keep her balance. She wanted to pour over both of them and fill their mouths with her cunt and her ass.

The orgasm caught her completely by surprise. It rose up fast and furious, hot and slinky, and seemed to wrap around her the same way Charlotte and Liz had their tongues wrapped around her crotch. One moment she was enjoying the rich sensation of their mouths on her, and the next, she was lost in the power of her climax, gasping and crying. The flood broke over her, but the two kneeling at her feet did not stop what they were doing. Suddenly she realized that there was a second rush, and moments after the first orgasm had fled through her, she came again, this time even more explosively than the first. Charlotte and Liz rode it all the way through, their mouths on her trembling flesh as she screamed out in her excitement.

When it was all finished, she could hardly find the strength to make her way over to the bed and lie down it. Her limbs refused to obey her commands and she collapsed on the sheets, completely spent. She hadn't experienced anything like that in a long time and she stayed with it, still moaning. Every few seconds a hot shudder went through her and she gave herself over to it.

"I think we broke her," Charlotte laughed.

"Well, she doesn't look like she'll be much good for anything right now," Liz said. "We might as well start without her and let her catch up."

Still kneeling on the floor, the two women moved closer together until they could hug and kiss. Their tongues met and they continued like that, their hands touching each other, running over breasts and teasing at pussies.

With some effort, Robin lifted her head and watched them. It was almost like watching a dance as their hands moved over each other in harmony. Each was now sitting with her legs apart, and each had her hand in the other's pussy. Both of them were already very wet, and their fingers slipped effortlessly in the damp pink recesses.

As satisfied as she was, Robin was almost immediately turned on by seeing them feeling each other's cunts, and as she watched, her own pussy stirred again with want and need.

It had been a long time since Charlotte and Liz had enjoyed each other, but the years fell away as they touched. They remembered favorite places and special touches, and applied these to each other freely. Liz put her free hand to Charlotte's pussy and put the other one in her mouth so she could suck the sweet juice off her fingers. Robin couldn't stay on the bed any longer, and she joined them on the floor. Charlotte offered her hand, and Robin tasted Liz's heat from the fingers of her own lover.

The two were far enough apart that Robin could finally get to those huge nipples that she had coveted. Liz groaned as she felt Robin's ruby lips on them, and Robin gasped herself as the big nubs filled her mouth. She sucked in first one and then the other, kneading the breasts with her fingers while she did. She blew gently on them to make the wet skin go cold, and then plunged them into her hot mouth. Liz moaned aloud, and Charlotte took the opportunity to rub her thumb hard on her clit.

It didn't take much more than that, and with her tits and her pussy so well looked after, Liz gave herself up to the orgasm that spread throughout her. She was very noisy, and Charlotte encouraged her until she was screaming out with the joy she felt. Robin shivered warmly at the sound; she loved to see another woman enjoying herself so thoroughly.

"Still a screamer, I see," Charlotte teased, and Robin was surprised at herself. Instead of feeling jealous and left out, she felt even closer to this huge-nippled, sensual woman. She wanted to make her come again, to feel those tits in her mouth, to hear those screams of delight when she climaxed.

Charlotte was now the only one who had not come, and both Robin and Liz were anxious to rectify that. They worked together, their ideas almost the same even though they exchanged no words. They didn't even bother to put her on the bed, for they were too anxious; instead, Robin had Charlotte lie on her stomach on the thick carpet, while Liz slipped two pillows under her belly. Her ass was raised, her glistening pussy exposed from behind.

Robin now had the fun of coming on to her lover just as Charlotte had done to her. Her tongue played down the crack of Charlotte's ass, leaving wet streaks on the creamy skin, while Liz, lying flat on the floor between Charlotte's legs, used her fingers and tongue to stroke and play with Charlotte's pussy.

They worked her over as a team. When Liz was busy on Charlotte's clit, Robin slipped two fingers into the sweet wet hole and used them to fuck her partner. Then Liz moved up to fill Charlotte's tunnel with her tongue, and Robin used her other hand to explore the opening to Charlotte's sweet ass.

It didn't take long before their teamwork produced the desired results. Within a few minutes, Charlotte was gasping and writhing, pushing her ass higher to take in both of them and crying with the pleasure. When she came with Robin's fingers in her cunt, Robin could feel the muscles tighten around her, trying to suck her in. All three of them rode out the orgasm until it was finally over and Charlotte was left panting on the carpet.

She rolled over and the other two lay down beside her, one on each side, running their hands over her and sharing sweet tiny kisses.

"It's a shame you two have to go back so soon," Liz said, as she reached down to cup Charlotte's wet pussy with her hand.

"Well...," Robin said, slowly, "I guess my assistant manager's pretty confident with what she's doing."

"And it would be a pretty sorry state of affairs if I couldn't tell them I'm taking some time off," Charlotte said. "Liz, where's the phone?"

"In the living room," Liz smiled, "right under the painting. But can't it wait for a little while?"

"And the trip to the sand dunes?"

"They've been there a million years," Liz said, as she reached across to stroke first Charlotte's belly and then Robin's. "I think we can safely say they'll still be there tomorrow."

Chapter Nine

Nora

"Nora. That's such a pretty name." The name of the woman sitting across the table was Kate Silvers, and Nora was transfixed by her.
They were sitting in a bar, one that had been highly recommended to Nora by Charlotte West. For years

Nora had wanted to find a gay bar, in the hopes that she could meet a woman who would fulfill her lesbian fantasies, but she hadn't had a clue how to find one. Now it turned out that there had been one just a few blocks from her home. Even with the knowledge, and with several sexual encounters with Charlotte and Robin behind her, it was still difficult to get up the nerve to actually enter the bar. On several evenings she dressed and then sat on the sofa and stayed there; on a few more, she walked down the street but kept going right past the door, too nervous to actually open it. Many times she sat in her car across the street, watching for hours as women went in or came out. She could get no further than putting her hand on the door handle of the car; she couldn't bring herself to actually open it and get out.

Finally she decided that it was time to stop being silly and to take control of her new life. This evening, she had stopped, taken a deep breath, and pulled open the door to the bar. When she stepped through it, she felt as if she were moving slowly through water. The blood pounded in her ears and she actually felt dizzy for a moment.

Then her eyes adjusted to the dim lights and she looked around. Amazingly, it looked no different from any bar she had been in before, except that all of the patrons and the staff were women. She didn't know exactly what she had been expecting—perhaps women making love on the tables, or crude dykes in motorcycle jackets terrorizing young virginal women. She did know, however, that this bar was nothing like what she had pictured.

Trying to act as cool as possible, she sat down at a small table. It was difficult, for her stomach was in knots, and she had to take a deep breath and try to stop her hands from shaking. A waitress came over and took her order for bourbon and water. When the drink came, she sipped at it, still nervous, still unsure where to look. Every time she picked up the glass, she thought she might drop it. She knew why she was here, but still she didn't want to catch anyone's eye. She didn't want to be a hunter, but at the same time, she didn't want to feel hunted either. She was looking for equal ground.

Eventually she got it. She was working on her second bourbon when a woman came by and looked at the empty seat on the other side of the table. "Are you waiting for someone?" she asked.

"No, I'm not," Nora replied.

"Mind if I sit down then?"

Hardly daring to believe her own newfound calm, Nora said, "Please do," and watched as her new companion made herself comfortable.

Kate Silvers, as she introduced herself, appeared to be just what Nora had been looking for. She was cheerful with an infectious smile, just a little plump, with long wavy red hair and the complexion that went with it. Her large gray eyes sparkled when she talked, and she seemed very carefree and friendly. In just a few minutes, Nora felt like she was sitting at the kitchen table with an old friend sharing coffee, instead of at a table in a gay bar trying to find someone to share sex. She felt comfortable with Kate, and very shortly she was laughing and joking as well. The nervousness had passed completely, thanks to this captivating young woman.

Kate had shattered another illusion that Nora had of dour lesbians taking everything seriously. Nora could imagine having sex with Kate very easily, and it seemed that it would be less of a performance than a joyous romp. The more she thought about it, the more she found herself attracted to this pleasant woman who sat sipping at her rum and cola. And the more she talked and drank in this exhilarating woman, the more her pussy began to tell her that her experiences with Charlotte and Robin were not the end of her foray into this lifestyle she had longed to enter for so long. She wanted Kate. She wanted Kate very badly.

Little did she know, in her ignorance, that Kate wanted her just as much. At this point, her inexperience led her to miss the subtle looks, the tone of Kate's musical voice, and especially the way she glanced at Nora's tits, firm and perky under her thin shirt. She might never have known it, except that Kate put down her glass and reached across the table to put her hand on Nora's wrist. Her fingers were warm, almost hot, and Nora felt the imprint of her fingers long after Kate took her hand away. She was surprised that the fingertips didn't leave a mark, for she could still feel them there. Just the touch of a sexually attractive woman was enough to set her off, or so it seemed. She might have moaned aloud. At any rate, she had to squeeze her thighs tightly together in the hopes of relieving just a little of the pressure that was building up in the hot folds of her cunt.

"This is a nice bar," Kate said, "but I find their

prices are a little steep. Do you want to come back to my apartment? I have some wine there that we can enjoy without spending half our paychecks." It took Nora a few seconds to realize the implications behind the offer, but when she did, she was almost giddy with need and hot desire. "Of course," she said, and drained her glass quickly. She put it down just as fast, hoping that her haste hadn't given her away or appeared rude. She relaxed visibly when Kate finished her own drink in two quick gulps. It was obvious, Nora thought, that she was wanted by this woman just as much as she desired to feel that rich flesh under her fingers.

"Come on, then," Kate said, and she put on her jacket; Nora followed her out of the bar. She could hardly believe she was doing it. Imagine, Nora Stevens going into a gay bar and then leaving a short time later with another woman! A few months ago—before her unbelievable good luck at being invited out with Charlotte and Robin—it might have been a dream, to be broken by the unwelcome intrusion of waking. Now it was a lovely reality.

Kate's car was in the parking lot, a nondescript sedan that had a plastic coffee cup stuck to the dash and some clothes, not yet dropped off at the dry cleaner's, tossed on the back seat. Nora liked it. Charlotte and Robin were very well-off, always perfectly turned out and exquisitely dressed; their spotless cars were expensive luxury models, their home was a showcase. Nora adored being part of that world when she was with them, but she also firmly believed in the importance of diversity. Kate's earthiness was so different from them, and she knew it would have to show in her lovemaking. She felt like a virgin again, discovering sex for the first time.

Kate lived not too far from the bar, in a small, well-kept apartment building. It was an older, restored building, with small balconies outlined in wrought iron, and several people were enjoying the warm evening sitting on them with cool drinks in their hands. Nora thought she would be embarrassed, but to her surprise, she felt elated as she walked to the door with Kate, watched with mild interest by the tenants. She felt deeply sensual and wondered if any of them knew her purpose there. Secretly she hoped they would.

As Nora had expected, Kate's apartment was lived-in, cozy, and comfortable. She felt completely relaxed as she sat down on the sofa, patting the head of the huge orange cat that shared it with her. Kate busied herself in the kitchen and shortly afterwards came out with two glasses of chilled wine.

They sat together on the sofa, and for a moment, Nora felt a quick burst of panic—she didn't know this woman at all, didn't know what to talk about. It passed almost immediately as Kate lifted her glass and took a sip, then started talking about a restaurant she had visited the previous week and how good their lasagna was. Nora felt like she had finally come home.

It was only natural, then, that when Kate leaned over and kissed her, that she returned it lovingly and happily. It was as if an old friend that she'd long admired had come forth as a lesbian, wanting love and sex. Nora had been waiting to kiss those lips for years.

Kate's tongue was hot and rich. She took Nora's glass from her without breaking away and set it down, then used her hands to caress Nora's throat. Nora hugged her hard, and without any thought, her fingers found Kate's breasts through her shirt. They were soft and pillowy and Nora squeezed them. She could feel the nipples huge and hard under the fabric.

"I can't wait for you any longer," Kate whispered, and she took Nora's hand and led her into the bedroom. It was as cozy as the living room, the bed clean but invitingly rumpled. They fell onto it together, smoothly, their hands still on each other even though they hadn't even undressed. They were having too much fun with their tongues in each other's mouths, their fingers exploring through their clothes.

Nora's slim, hard body was a lovely contrast to Kate's soft, yielding one, and each was fascinated with the other. Kate loosened the buttons of Nora's blouse and pulled it away so that the neat, firm tits were exposed. She lost no time in putting her hot mouth over them, and Nora's groan was heartfelt and sincere. It was both the thrill that went through her nipples and the sight of this redheaded new friend together that did it.

She helped Kate to undress her completely. There was no nervousness when she was completely naked, for Kate was admiring, running her hands over the firm flesh. Then both turned their attention to Kate's clothing. When they were both naked, Nora just had to hug her fully, pressing her body against her partner. It felt so good just to touch completely and enjoy the warmth of Kate's skin. Kate's ruddy pubic hair was hot against her own, and Kate's soft breasts almost melted against her own. Nora again surprised herself by taking the initiative and slipping her hand between Kate's thighs. Her fingers were wet as soon as she touched the pussy that waited for her. She knew that hers was just as soaked, and when Kate put her hand down there moments later, her fingers were hot and sticky as well.

Kate pulled away then, and dipped her fingers into the cleft of Nora's cunt again until they were well covered with Nora's hot pussy juice. She spread it over Nora's hard nipples until they were shiny with the sweet nectar. Then she licked it off, so slowly that Nora begged her to take her right then. Nora felt like her tits and her cunt were connected and every touch of Kate's pink tongue on her nipples was a shot of white-hot pleasure pouring down to her clit. She groaned with the dull, rich ache between her legs.

They rolled over, clasped in each other's arms, and then Nora found herself on the bottom, with Kate moving over her. Within moments that reddish pussy was over her lips. She was consumed with hunger for it and she took it eagerly. She grabbed Kate's asscheeks and pulled her cunt down, so that she was surrounded by it.

The taste was wine-rich and sweet and Nora thought of hot burgundy. Kate was gasping, moaning, actually laughing as Nora's tongue filled her. She loved sex, loved to be eaten, loved to come. It was contagious and Nora pushed her tongue deep into Kate's tight hole. She wanted to get right inside.

Kate's hands were working their own magic between Nora's legs. She slipped her fingers inside Nora's pussy and once they were wet, she slid them effortlessly across the hot moist flesh. She rubbed the channels alongside Nora's clit and then massaged the hard knot in the middle. Nora gasped. When Kate put her other hand deep between Nora's legs, using her fingertip to carefully tease the tight rosebud of Nora's ass, it was divine.

"Eat me, sweetie!" Kate begged, and Nora obliged, squeezing Kate's delicious thighs and sinking her fingers into the skin, then pulling Kate closer to her. She was drowning in this woman's cunt. Her lips were soaked, her cheeks were hot with pussyjuice, and still she couldn't get enough.

Neither could Kate. She was on fire and Nora was stoking it even more. She writhed on Nora's tongue, using her almost like a dildo as she slid her pussy over Nora's mouth. She ground herself on her, wanting it harder and deeper, and Nora gave it to her. They were moving together now, tongue and cunt, mouth and clit.

She cried out and groaned hard as each touch pushed her even higher. When she finally reached the edge and was swept out over it, she all but screamed. Nora kept up with her and licked her hard right until her orgasm was finished, and when Kate moved away, she was gasping but smiling broadly.

"Damn, you are good!" she said, as she tried to catch her breath. Little tremors went through her as she lay beside her new lover, and Nora reached out and tickled Kate's pussy to prolong them. "I'm sorry, but I just had to come. You are exciting, Nora, don't ever let anyone tell you differently. I haven't come that hard in ages."

"Don't be sorry," Nora said, trying hard to keep from beaming with pride at Kate's words. "I just hope you're planning on doing the same for me," she continued. She was teasing, but both of them knew she was serious as well. The throbbing between her legs was almost unbearable and Kate's fingers on her had only served to increase her tension. She had to come!

"Let me show you then," Kate said, and she left the room. She returned quickly, carrying a glass almost filled with wine.

She had Nora lie flat on the bed and knelt over her. She took a drink of the wine and then kissed her deeply. Nora relished her cool tongue and the rich taste of the wine as she pushed her own tongue into Kate's mouth.

Then Kate broke away and held the glass over Nora's breasts. Tipping it up, she dribbled a bit onto the sweet hard nipples. Nora gasped at the cold liquid splashing on her warm skin. Then she sighed happily as she felt Kate's hot mouth on her, licking it up. Once the wine was gone, Kate spent a long time circling each nipple and reaching under Nora's breasts to slowly lick at the half-circle under each one.

Next, she slowly dripped wine between her breasts and licked dry the soft skin separating them. She dribbled the cold wine down below them and then on her belly, each time accompanied by Nora's sharp intake of breath and then the quiet sigh as her hot tongue lapped over skin to clean the wine away.

Finally the glass was poised over the blonde hair at her crotch, and Nora held her breath, waiting. Kate knew how excited she was, and she moved the glass ever so slowly, letting the golden liquid lap at the rim before she finally let it fall.

Nora gasped as the wine hit her mound. It moved in a cold river into the cleft, splashed over her clit and made its way down to the hot tunnel. It soaked her thighs and her asscheeks and her whole pussy felt cold. She could hardly wait for Kate to warm it.

Kate's breath was hot against it, but nowhere near as explosive as the fire of her tongue. Nora cried out as it touched her pussy and lapped up the wine that glittered like drops of dew on her cunthairs.

"Lick my cunt!" she heard herself say, and the words sounded so natural coming out of her mouth. Kate did, with long, slow laps that started at her hot tunnel and worked their way up to the hard clit that peeked out from between her lips.

She let more wine fall as she was licking, and Nora was treated to the unique sensation as the cold wine and the hot tongue met at the same time on her pussy. It was delightful, the warm and cool together, the hot shivers and the cold chills that ran throughout her whole body together.

She propped herself up so that she could see. Kate was between her legs, looking up at her, and those huge gray eyes were smiling. This was not serious sex, this was fun. This was the romp that Nora had longed for, and it had come true. She fell back and let the whole experience wash right over her.

Her climax flooded over her just the same way moments later. It began deep in her pussy, but took on a life of its own as it rushed through her. To her surprise, when she cried out, there was laughter in it also. It seemed as if Kate inspired it. Indeed, the redheaded woman stayed tightly between her legs, her tongue on the swollen, pulsating clit, licking every last tremor out of it. When it had finally passed, she lapped widely over Nora's whole pussy several times to get the last taste of the juice that had seeped out. Mixed with the wine, it was an intoxicating cocktail.

They lay together in each other's arms, sharing what remained of the wine in the glass. Nora couldn't hug Kate tightly enough, and Kate returned the embrace gladly. Her kisses were sweet with Nora's nectar and the wine, and Nora pushed her tongue in deep to get every trace of it.

"You're going to get me started again," Kate warned.

"I know," Nora said, as she kissed her companion again and again. "Oh, I know."

Chapter Ten

Astra

Astra looked at the clock on the wall, checked it against her watch—a habit she'd had for more years than she could count—and fumed. Where the hell was she!

She paced back and forth through her studio, adjusting something each time. She pulled the backdrop to tighten it a little and pushed one of the lights over a quarter of an inch. She looked through the viewfinder on the camera and then checked the clock and her watch again. Ten minutes late! Who did this bitch think she was?

She was brusque with the equipment and had to catch herself when she found she was being too rough with the camera. Her manner changed immediately, though, when she went over to the table where the props were kept.

Here she stopped and took her time. Each item was picked up, checked carefully, and then set down almost with reverence. There was a collar and a pair of cuffs. There was a body harness and a riding crop, a leash, some chains, a latex hood, a soft velour blindfold.

The company selling the jeans had contacted her and had told her they wanted something outrageous. Jeans were only selling well when they had really off-beat ads, they told her, and they wanted an angle that no other company had really covered. Astra knew that nostalgia, cowboys, and pickup trucks had been done to death. That company with the newborn babies and the smooching clergy had the shock angle all sewn up. Sex was also becoming a tired subject, except for one variation, and Astra knew it well.

When she had brought up the idea of domination, there had been silence on the other end of the line. Then, slowly, she talked them into it. Now she was waiting for her model, a little bitch who was now twelve minutes late and counting.

Astra continued to check her equipment. It was all

spotless, she knew; Margot had cleaned it several times over and had received a nasty spanking when Astra had found the tiniest fingerprint on the inside of a collar. She ran her fingernails over the spreader bar, then checked out the items at the back of the table. There was a pair of nasty gold nipple clamps, their ends securely joined together with a thin gold chain; there was a ball gag and a chrome-studded leather paddle. Astra didn't intend to use those in the photo shoot, of course, but at the same time she felt it didn't hurt to have them there. One never knew what might happen in the course of a shoot.

The model finally arrived fifteen minutes late, and Astra tried to control her fury. Through clenched teeth she said quietly, "Do you know what time it is?"

"I'm sorry, I really am. I couldn't get a cab," the young woman said as she took off her light jacket. It was a sincere excuse, sincerely given, and she lowered her eyes when she said it. Astra stood back then and looked her over appraisingly.

She was in her early twenties, tall and model-thin. Her hair was long and straight, light brown, gently streaked. Ever the professional, Astra silently and quickly sized up her huge eyes, her long eyelashes, her straight nose, her full pouty lips, making mental notes about the best way to light her. Her name, she said, was Shannon.

"Well, Shannon, didn't you learn about the importance of punctuality in modeling school?" It was a throwaway comment, made almost with no emotion and with no expectation of an answer; Astra was too busy looking the woman over and judging her shots. But Shannon was obviously upset about it, and she looked downcast and sulky, like a student awaiting punishment from her teacher.

Then Astra snapped to attention, standing in front of her model, getting her ready. She never took any attitude but one of dominance, whether it was sexual, business, or social. She was completely in charge here and she laid down the guidelines. Her models either accepted them or left; there was no middle ground.

"Did the agency tell you what I am expecting of you?" she asked.

"They told me it was unusual," Shannon replied.

"I think you'll find that an understatement," Astra said, but she didn't smile. She led Shannon over to the table where the restraints were laid out with the precision of surgical instruments. "The theme is going to be bondage and domination. You are going to be restrained, you are going to be displayed. You will be nude from the waist up. If you don't think you can handle it, then tell me now and I'll get someone else. Otherwise, get ready to work."

Shannon's eyes went wide as she took in the display on the table, and for a moment, Astra thought that the young woman was indeed going to grab her coat and run for the door. But Shannon's expression was a difficult one to read: surprise, intrigue and, it seemed to Astra, anticipation.

"I'm ready to work," Shannon said, and Astra breathed a sigh of relief—getting another model would mean a wasted day—and led her back across the room.

She ordered the young woman to undress. Shannon looked around in vain for a dressing room. "Where?" she asked.

Astra longed for a submissive instead of this creature. At least with a submissive she could have reached out and slapped her for asking such a stupid question. "Right here," she said. "You're going to be shot nude. I don't think this is the time for false modesty."

Shannon dropped her eyes again as she unbuttoned her blouse. Astra watched her with a cold professionalism, but at the same time her interest went beyond the perimeters of her work. Shannon's long neck and nicely rounded shoulders were sweet, but her firm small breasts were even better.

The nipples were well formed and peaked out beautifully, and they were perfectly situated on the perky small globes. Her belly was flat and her mound rose gently, covered with light brown hair. Her legs were long and shapely. Astra sized her up. The agency had outdone themselves on this one. This was material that she could work with, in more ways than one.

She had several pairs of the company's jeans in different styles and she selected one, then handed it over. The denim fit like a dream and clung to Shannon as if molded to her skin. Astra was now getting into the shot, setting it up in her mind. She walked over to the table and looked everything over.

She decided to begin simply, for two reasons. One was that she wanted to use as many variations as possible, so that the advertising agency could decide if it wanted to go for only the suggestion or for a full-blown demonstration. Secondly, she wasn't sure about her model and she wanted to break her in slowly. Deep inside, she wanted to break her completely.

She chose the blindfold, the collar, and the cuffs. Almost instinctively, she turned around to Shannon, who was standing watching her. "Kneel," she said.

"Pardon me?" Astra had to catch herself. She'd never done a shoot like this before and she reminded herself that it wasn't a submissive standing before her questioning her actions. Such a query would have received a backhand across the face, followed by the choosing of a suitable punishment. No, this was a professional model, who had no idea what was expected of women who wore these devices happily at the whim of their Mistress.

"Kneel on the floor, now," Astra said coldly, then added quickly, "It will get you in the mood so much quicker. You don't just wear these things, you know. This is a lifestyle, a whole new frame of mind."

"I have heard that," Shannon said, and quickly she dropped to her knees on the floor before Astra. When Astra opened the collar, Shannon seemed to thrust her throat forward, almost welcoming it. When the buckle was fastened at the back of her neck, she closed her eyes and smiled gently. Astra's heart beat a little quicker. What were the chances?

She set Shannon up against the backdrop and shot a number of pictures with just the collar. Then she added the blindfold. Shannon was more unsure once her eyes were covered, afraid to move about. Astra put her fingers under the collar and used it to direct her model's motions. Shannon relaxed and gave herself over completely to Astra's touch, a reaction not lost on the platinum-haired photographer.

Shannon was in Astra's absolute control. Although there wasn't anything around her that she could knock over or walk into—and she knew it—she did not move without the photographer's directions. Astra gave her commands quickly, biting off the words, and it seemed like Shannon was almost too eager to obey. When Astra touched her to move an arm or a leg into position, her chin dropped, almost submissively. Shannon was helpless and she knew it, but she was obeying more than her position required. Astra was elated.

When she took the blindfold off, Shannon was kneeling on the floor. She blinked, confused, and looked around almost in a daze; it took her a moment to realize where she was.

"How are you holding up?" Astra asked, her back to the young woman on the floor.

"Wonderful—," Shannon began, joyfully; then she corrected herself, and assumed a more professional attitude. "I'm fine. What else is there?"

It was time for the cuffs next, which Astra fastened about each small wrist. She noticed that Shannon's nipples were now achingly hard, standing out firmly from those perfect tits. She managed to brush one with her hand as she buckled the leather manacles around Shannon's arms. The young woman let the tiniest groan out and shivered visibly.

"Is this exciting you?" Astra asked. She was expecting no reply and was surprised when Shannon said, "Yes, I think it is."

"That's what I need to work with," Astra said. "You have felt the touch of these things on you. Now I want you to get inside the part you are playing. It will make the pictures believable. Do you understand?"

"Yes," Shannon said, almost in a whisper.

"Your first mistake," Astra said. "If you are submissive, then I am your dominatrix. You will address me as 'Mistress' at all times. Is that clear?"

"Yes—Mistress," Shannon said, and Astra felt a warm shudder go through her body. How she loved it when she heard that term come from a submissive's lips!

"You will do nothing unless you are told to do it, and when you are given a command, you will obey it immediately. Do you understand?"

"Yes, Mistress," Shannon whispered. She looked up at Astra and in her eyes the photographer thought she saw respect and even gratitude.

Almost roughly she pulled Shannon's arms behind her; those magnificent tits were thrust forward, the nipples straining against the skin. With a chrome clasp she tied the cuffs together. She took several photos, but there was something missing. The leash was snapped to the collar, and she allowed it to hang to the floor, swirling on the fabric of the backdrop. Then she took the riding crop. "Open your mouth," she ordered.

Shannon obeyed immediately, and Astra thrust the leather crop between her lips. "Hold it there," Astra ordered, and then she went back to the camera. The sight warmed her through. The tight denim, almost a restraint itself as it molded itself to Shannon's ass. The arms held together, the wrists crossed, secured by the metal rings. The outline of the outthrust breast, just the edge of the nipple visible. The smooth curve of Shannon's spine and the hair spread over it. The collar around the perfect throat, the leash appearing to have just been dropped by a Mistress. The riding crop held in the teeth, inevitably placed and held there by a command. She shivered as she pressed the button to capture it on film.

When she had everything she wanted, she took the crop from Shannon's mouth. Before she walked away, though, she pushed it back at the young woman. "Kiss it," she said.

"Mistress?"

"Kiss it," Astra repeated. "This crop can hurt you terribly, but you love and respect it when it does. Kiss it now. Respect it completely." Shannon did, forming her lips around the leather shaft as if she were taking a lover to her. Astra smiled.

She released Shannon's hands and then ordered her to take off the jeans. When she bent over, her back to Astra, the photographer could get a clear glimpse of her pussy. It was no surprise to Astra when she saw the glimmer of juice on the sweet lips. She had pegged this one correctly, it seemed.

This time she handed over a pair of shorts. This meant that she could use the spreader bar to its potential, and she did not miss the look on Shannon's face when she brought it over.

The spreader bar was a length of metal pipe, painted black, with two restraints on it set far apart. Shannon was ordered to stand with her legs parted and a restraint was buckled around each slim ankle. There were rings on the ends of the bar and Astra used the chains here. The sleek metal ran from these rings and attached to the cuffs on Shannon's wrists. She could not move at all without risking falling over.

Shannon was breathing heavily now, her full lips parted, her eyes closed tightly. "Is anything wrong?" Astra asked.

"Oh, no, Mistress!" Shannon said, and she smiled when she did. "Nothing is wrong, nothing at all!"

"Look at me," Astra ordered, and Shannon opened her eyes. "I'm going to ask you a question, and I expect an honest answer. Does this frighten you or does it excite you?"

Shannon breathed deeply again, and kept her eyes down as she answered. "I don't really know how to say this, Mistress," she said. "I have read about this, and I know that women like you exist. Women who can control other women. I have always had a desire to be under this control."

"I knew it as soon as you came in the door," Astra said.

Shannon was surprised. "Is it that obvious, Mistress?" she asked.

"Perhaps not to the untrained eye," Astra replied, "but to the dominatrix it is. You must consider yourself very fortunate. Many women go through their whole lives searching, but not knowing what it is they seek. You have found it."

"Yes," Shannon said, "and I am grateful, Mistress!" The conversation was over abruptly, as Astra returned to her role of photographer and went back to the camera. This time the images were superb. The restraints pulled Shannon's legs apart, outlining the long muscles in each and exposing her crotch. The shorts were so tight they only barely kept her pussy covered. Her tits were exposed, her hair was disheveled, her eyes were looking for her Mistress, expecting her punishment. If this didn't sell clothes... Astra decided that if these shots were used, every Mistress in town would be buying a pair for her slave.

Now she was determined to make this the ultimate shoot. She picked up the body harness, a bizarre contraption made of leather straps, bright chrome rings and buckles. The spreader bar was left in place, holding Shannon's legs out from each other, but the wrist cuffs and their chains were removed.

The straps crossed over Shannon's tits, and Astra pulled the buckles tight so that the globes stood out from the black leather. Straps went around her upper arms, holding them immobile beside her body. A protective strap was there to go between her legs, but Astra left this undone and hanging to show off the denim shorts. Shannon had her eyes closed again, breathing in the musky smell of the leather and enjoying the feeling of once again being completely helpless. The click of the shutter only added to her excitement.

Eventually the latex hood was put over her head. Astra was particularly fond of this one, for its shiny surface reflected the lights back into the lens. It made her model faceless, and she adjusted the lighting and Shannon's stance so that the clothing was prominent in the pictures. When she took it off, Shannon's face was red and her hair was plastered to her skin. The hoods were very hot and Astra enjoyed using them for especially cruel punishment.

Astra now had all the pictures she wanted, but she did not tell Shannon this. Instead, she loosened the young woman from the harness and the spreader bar and ordered her to take the shorts off. Now that her work was done, she could admire Shannon's naked body in a different light, and she liked what she saw. "Now," she said, "you've worn the devices and you've been bound."

"Thank you, Mistress," Shannon said, her voice heavy with gratitude.

"Of course," Astra continued, "that is only the beginning when one is in the control of a dominatrix. You do know that there is more, don't you?"

"Yes, Mistress," Shannon whispered.

"It begins," Astra said, "with the fact that you were fifteen minutes late."

For the first time, Shannon's intrigue turned to fear. Her eyes went wide as the full implications came to her, but from experience, Astra knew that there was no dread there. She had found one that she could work with.

"I tried to be on time, Mistress," Shannon said. Astra's response was a slap across the face, so fast that Shannon never saw it coming. Immediately her hand went to her face, the shock in her eyes.

"If I wanted an excuse, I would have asked for it," Astra replied coldly. "Now on your knees." Shannon obeyed immediately.

She didn't see Astra come up behind her. All she felt was her Mistress' strong hands at her lips, forcing her mouth open, and then the harsh rubber taste as a ball gag was stuffed into her mouth. She whimpered as the buckle was fastened securely at the back of her head. It was very uncomfortable, for the ball forced her lips open wide. But even though she was not confined, she stayed on her knees, accepting it. It was what she had wanted for so long, and it was finally happening to her.

She wasn't entirely sure when she saw Astra pick up the nipple clamps, the pair held together by a thin gold chain. She whimpered through the gag and shook her head as Astra's fingers opened the cruel clips. Nevertheless she stayed on her knees, right where her Mistress had ordered her to be.

Astra smiled when she stood before her gagged submissive. "This is for the first five minutes I waited," she said, and she grabbed Shannon's tit and squeezed it so that the nipple was outstretched. Then she snapped the clamp closed on it. She could hear Shannon's scream through the gag, and she watched as the young woman screwed her eyes tightly closed. She knew that she was fighting nausea and the pain as she knelt, trying to breathe deeply and calmly through her nose.

Astra waited until she had gained her composure before she grabbed Shannon's other tit. "This is for the second five minutes," she said, and again Shannon had to deal with the searing fire that went through her chest as the metal clip compressed the tender soft nub of her nipple.

The chain hung between them, glittering softly

under the hot camera lights. Astra ran it between her fingers and when Shannon calmed down, she tugged at it gently. Even a touch that light was enough to send Shannon off again. "I hope you will remember this lesson for a long time," she said. "I can think of no Mistress anywhere who will tolerate tardiness. I certainly know that I won't."

There were tears at the corners of Shannon's eyes, and her nipples were fiery red. Using the chain, Astra forced her down to her hands and knees. She ran her fingers over the silky smooth buttocks; she always enjoyed the feeling of female flesh and this was especially nice. The exposed pussy was wet and Astra ran her fingers over it as well. Shannon shuddered at the touch on her cunt. Astra wiped her wet fingers on Shannon's asscheeks, admiring the shiny smear.

It was the spot she chose with the studded paddle. Her first strike was relatively gentle, and Shannon's reaction was more of surprise. She hadn't been given permission to turn around, and so had not known what was coming. Nevertheless, it was a stinging blow and it raised red marks on the creamy skin.

The next was harder, and the one after harder still, until Astra was smacking the paddle down with most of her strength. The welts it raised were delicious, and Shannon's whole ass was mottled red. She gave four to each side, and then brought the paddle's cruel face down over both, until Shannon was weeping.

Finally Astra brought the paddle down a final time, and walked across the room to put it away. She left Shannon like that for a long time, without permission to move. The young woman stayed on her hands and knees, tears streaming down her face, her mouth distorted by the rubber ball. Astra turned off the bright lights and put the camera away and by the time she came back to the young model on the floor, the studio was completely cleaned up.

She pulled Shannon up by the chain attached to the nipple clamps, and Shannon's eyes were wide with pain and fear. Astra had a bold desire to pull them off with the chain, but decided against it; cruelty of that degree could wait for another day. Even so, opening the clips carefully and removing them gently was still painful as the feeling came back into the bruised nubs. Shannon thought her chest was burning up.

She moved her jaw slowly and stiffly when the ball gag was finally removed, but she did not say anything. She stayed on her knees, hoping that Astra would not order her to sit down on those poor bruised asscheeks.

"I believe that you will not be a half a minute late next time," Astra said.

"No, Mistress," Shannon said, and tried to control her jubilation. There would be a next time! She wanted to shout with joy.

"You realize," Astra said, "that you are as green a submissive as any I have ever seen. Naturally I know it is because this is your first time. I can accept that. I cannot accept a submissive who will not learn what is expected of her."

"No, Mistress," Shannon said.

"Then you will be here tomorrow at, say, ten o'clock promptly?"

"Ten promptly, Mistress," Shannon beamed.

"Then get dressed and get out of here," Astra said. "I have work to do."

The young model got up quickly and grabbed her clothes. She could hardly dress fast enough in her desire to please her Mistress, even if she did stop a moment at the door and look longingly at the table covered with the instruments of torture that she would become so familiar with.

Astra watched her go and smiled. She had not thanked her Mistress for the permission to get dressed. All things in time, she thought, and picked up the riding crop. It whistled through the air delightfully. Tomorrow, Astra thought, it would find its mark. She could hardly wait.

Chapter Eleven

Carly and Margot

Margot held her breath as Carly lifted up the tail of her loose knit shirt. This was always her very favorite part, when Carly's tits were exposed to her.

It wasn't just the tits themselves, although they were

full and soft, perfect for squeezing and for playing with, for sucking into one's mouth and teasing with a tongue. What she loved were the tiny gold rings, one through each nipple, and the star and the moon indelibly cast into the skin above the right one. Margot, conservative and gentle, longed for such decorations on herself, but could not imagine lying still and actually having it done. Through Carly she got her chance to enjoy them fully.

She was so frequently dominated by other women, by strong women who bound her in wrist cuffs and strapped her creamy ass firmly with cruel leather paddles when she disobeyed them—or sometimes even when she did obey, just for the pleasure of the punishment. She enjoyed that, but she also enjoyed her relationship with Carly, both of them equal, both of them lovers. She took one of the nipple rings between her teeth. The brassy taste was almost sweet.

Margot was herself naked, and Carly reached out to take Margot's own nipples in her fingers. The two women were almost exact opposites. Margot was tall, willowy, fine-boned and fine-featured, her thick hair luxurious and long. Carly was much shorter, stockier, her breasts much fuller. Her hair was cut very short, almost shorn, and dyed red, at least at this particular moment. Each thoroughly enjoyed the contrast.

They were together in Carly's loft, one of the more eccentric places Margot had ever had reason to visit. Being an artist, Carly wanted to live in the manner that was expected of her. The difference was that she was a rather successful artist and had much more money at her disposal than most people in her profession. She also liked creature comforts, so she used her money to combine the austere artist's life with the luxuries she loved so much. Her loft consisted of the two upper floors of a huge warehouse. The walls were unfinished, sandblasted brick and exposed pipes, as most of the artists' lofts were. But Carly's floors were mirror-finished hardwood, her enormous bathroom contained a whirlpool bath, and most of the furniture was antique. That included her king-sized bed, a heavy brass frame with a canopy that held mosquito netting. Margot liked to be inside it, surrounded by the white gauze.

Right now, they were on the daybed, which was so large that it was almost a double bed in itself. Carly had asked Margot to come up to her loft, and the young woman had torn herself away from her veterinary office as quickly as she could. On her own, her life was generally calm and orderly. In Carly she found a wild side that she felt was lacking in herself and she welcomed every opportunity to give in to it.

As for Carly, Margot was her calming effect. She enjoyed a wide range of lovers, most of them as outlandish as she. She enjoyed the company of dykes, which for her were the women who loved their sex hard and fast. With Margot she could be slow, gentle, romantic. The netting on the bed had been Margot's idea, taken from a magazine. Carly was now completely smitten with it and always slept inside its folds as if in the arms of a lover.

"I bought something yesterday," Carly said. It was almost a groan, for Margot's lips were still on her nipple, tugging gently at the gold ring.

"Do tell," Margot said in a muffled voice; her mouth never left the treat she had found.

"Let me go get it," Carly said, and tried to get up. Margot wouldn't let her. The tip of her tongue was now through the nipple ring, and her fingers were between Carly's legs. Carly was wet already, and Margot slipped a finger into the hot tunnel expertly.

The red-haired woman allowed Margot to push her back onto the daybed. The purchase could wait. Margot's long, slim fingers explored Carly's hot cunt eagerly until they were wet with pussyjuice, which Margot slowly sucked from them. Carly loved to watch her do that.

Carly felt like her whole pussy was liquid. Her skin seemed to mold itself to Margot's fingers, like she was sucking Margot's hand right up into herself. Now, bending over her, Margot was placing one well-formed breast between Carly's legs. She used the nipple to brush up and down on Carly's sex-swollen clit, to their mutual pleasure. The nipple slid over the wet pinkness as smoothly as a sigh.

"Your pussy is so beautiful," Margot said, as she moved her whole body back and forth to rub her tit on the sleek flesh. "I could sit here and play with it all day."

"You could," Carly sighed, "and I would let you. But I did buy something I think we can both have some fun with."

"In a minute," Margot said. "I can't stop now." She moved back between Carly's legs and with her hands, spread them apart even further. Then she put her head right beside that delicious cunt. The hair was trimmed and dyed the same outrageous shade of red as the hair on Carly's head. It was a game Carly played, and she had not forgotten the look on Margot's face when she had undressed in front of her several months ago. She had decided on a mixture of bright blue and yellow for her head, and had treated her pube to the same combination.

The color didn't matter at all right now. Margot had only one intention, and she snaked out her tongue to part the sweet lips and reach the treasure under them. It was honey sweet and hot as always. Margot wondered when there would be a tiny ring between these lips to tease with the tip of her tongue. It was something she had started longing for even if she didn't know exactly why.

Right now, though, everything she needed was here. She rimmed the entrance to Carly's hole with her tongue and then thrust it deep inside as if it were a kiss. Carly loved the full wet feeling and she pressed Margot into her. She wanted to swallow this woman whole.

She let Margot suck on her cunt for some time. The chills it sent through her were heavenly, but finally she could wait no longer to show off her purchase. She sat up and pulled Margot up to her, sharing a deep, rich kiss with the willowy woman as she did. Then she made her sit on the daybed while she went off to collect her delight, hidden under the bed, across the room.

She brought back the large box to the daybed, knelt

on the thick Oriental carpet, and told Margot to close her eyes and not to peek while she opened the box.

Margot was completely taken when she was allowed to open her eyes again, and she just stared, her mouth open.

"It's a rider," Carly said, as she showed off the device.

That was certainly the word for it. It was a large, contoured cushion, meant to be straddled as it sat on the floor. What made it different was the accessory on it. Pointing up from the seat was a huge dildo.

Margot sat down on the floor and ran her hands over it. It had a thick knob on the top, which she felt all over with her fingers, and veins running through it so that it looked realistic. Both in length and width it was massive, and the soft plastic felt warm in her hands. It was certainly a toy to be reckoned with.

"It's amazing," she said. She couldn't take her fingers off the shaft that pointed up, begging for a pussy to sit on it.

"I've seen them in catalogues many times," Carly said. Like Margot, she couldn't keep her hands away from the amazing device. "When I was in the leather shop, I overheard someone ordering one and I knew I had to have one. I thought you'd appreciate it. I certainly know I will."

"Let me try it out," Margot said, getting up to put herself on the plastic knob.

Carly stopped her, a hand on her wrist. "Will you indulge me?"

Margot looked at her, puzzled, but she smiled broadly. "What's your pleasure?"

Carly looked almost bashful, a reaction Margot never thought she would see in her outgoing, outlandish lover. "When I got it, I could just see you sitting on it. I could just imagine the way you would take that knob into your pussy and move down on it until that shaft was all the way inside you."

"So what would you like?" Carly closed her eyes and breathed deeply; she wasn't gathering the nerve to ask the question, she was completely lost in the ecstasy of asking it. "I would like to shave you," she said. "I want to see it going into you completely naked. I want to see every movement, every touch of it on you."

She opened her eyes quickly. "Of course, if you don't want to—"

Margot smiled. "I hope you have plenty of shaving cream," she said. "There's nothing worse than getting nicked down there, I'm sure."

Carly led her to the bathroom. Margot was always amazed by this room, for it was so unlike anything she would expect to find in a loft. She had seen so many movies where the facilities in such an apartment consisted of a toilet and basin out in the open.

Carly, on the other hand, didn't see it that way. For any crudeness she had elsewhere, she was very particular about her toilet habits and she had a passion for fancy bathrooms that few could match. She had spent a great deal of money, but she had exactly what she wanted.

It was a room of its own, huge, with a window that flooded the area with light. There was a copper-lined footed bathtub for long soaks and a shower with glass doors. There was a toilet and a bidet, and a sink set with a handmade enamel basin and elegant brass fittings. In one corner was the whirlpool bath with its delightful jets, which Margot had often pointed at her pussy with orgasmic results. The bathroom was so big that it held three chairs and a cupboard almost overflowing with thick bath sheets.

This was not a spur-of-the-moment question. On the table beside one of the chairs was a shaving kit, neatly set out. There was a mug of shaving cream and a brush, a comb, scissors, a razor and blades. The chair was protected by a thin plastic sheet and there was a bowl for warm water. Margot could imagine Carly getting everything ready. Indeed, while Carly had been setting it out—even including a linen napkin beneath everything on the table—the excitement had been enough to set her pussy throbbing and she had had to stop halfway through and use her fingers to make herself come.

Carly now sat Margot down in the chair, her legs spread wide, and almost reverently she kissed the hairy lips before she proceeded. First came the scissors, and she snipped the dark pubic hair away until only a short bristle remained. Margot was tense at first, but gradually she relaxed; she had complete faith in Carly's abilities with the scissors and the razor. The cold touch of the metal against her was exciting itself.

Now she took the brush and used it to whip the shaving cream in the mug. It was thick and rich and smelled almost spicy. She used the brush to mound the cream on Margot's pussy. It was warm and the brush tickled; Margot sighed and moved forward in the chair so that Carly could soap all of her.

Carly spent a long time doing this, for she loved the sight of Margot's pussy all fluffy and white with the thick cream. At one point she turned the brush around and probed into the white mound with the handle. Margot groaned as the ivory handle pushed against her clit. The shaving cream made her whole pussy tingle, a new and delightful experience. Even when it stung slightly on her clit, it was still a sweet sensation. She could imagine being completely covered in it, her whole body as white as her cunt.

She couldn't help tensing up at the first touch of the razor against her skin. Carly had warmed it in the water first, but there was still the involuntary reaction—this was a horrendously sharp steel blade taking the hair away from the most vulnerable part of her body. As with the scissors, though, the tension passed very quickly. A dominatrix might have nicked her just on principle. Carly, she knew, would not hurt her.

It was an unusual sensation. Carly used short strokes, cleaning the razor often. It was difficult to scrape the thick hair away and she had to pass over the skin several times until it was smooth. Margot could feel it, the razor catching on the hairs at first, and then eventually gliding over the skin. She looked down. Carly had cleaned all of the hair off her mound and was working her way down to the cream-covered lips. The skin was pale and it looked unusual without the hair, but the sight of it excited Margot as much as it did Carly. She had never been shaved before. It would be a new experience for them both.

It was much more difficult to take the razor over the

curves and folds of Margot's pussylips. Carly worked at it slowly, carefully. She used her fingers to stretch the skin and Margot sighed at the touch on this most sensitive area. The contrast between Carly's warm hands and the cool razor was intoxicating. Even the inherent danger of the sharp blade excited her.

When Margot's cuntlips were silky smooth, Carly shaved the insides of her thighs and all the way down to her sweet asshole, should any stray hairs be lurking there. When the job was finished, she took a thick towel and wiped away the last of the shaving cream, then she gave Margot a hand mirror so that she might admire the job.

Margot couldn't stop looking. She had never seen herself this way before, so young looking, so clean, so smooth. She held the lips together until her pussy was just a straight line between her legs. Then she spread it with her fingers and admired her large clit and the inner folds that were exposed. Her own touch on her skin was magical. Without any hair in the way she felt completely naked.

Carly finished the job by using her tongue on this newly shaved area. Margot almost cried out. It was unlike any tonguing she had ever received before. There was no barrier, just hot tongue on hot cunt, smooth mouth on hairless pussy. She almost came with just a few long, slow laps.

Carly wasn't about to give in that easily, though. "Come on," she said, taking Margot's hand. "We have a toy to play with, remember?"

In the excitement of the shaving Margot had completely forgotten Carly's "rider." Now she felt as if she were a different woman approaching it. The first time she had been a novice. This time she had been carefully prepared for what was to come. She thought of herself almost like a bride dressed and preened for the occasion, being led toward her wedding night.

Carly sank to the floor beside the device and touched her tongue to the tip of the knob. Margot watched, wanting her desperately as she did. Carly sucked it for Margot's benefit, wrapping her tongue around the shaft and taking it into her mouth.

"Suck it off!" Margot whispered, kneeling down on the thick carpet beside her. "Suck it off like you want to make it come." Carly began serious sucking on the monstrous dick. Margot wrapped her hand around the base of it, and with her other hand, played with the rings in Carly's nipples. She couldn't keep her eyes off Carly and the dildo in her mouth. Carly, meanwhile, kept glancing admiringly at Margot's sweet hairless cunt. She had had hairless women before, many times, but she had never actually shaved anyone before. It was sweet to look at her own handiwork.

The dildo was now glistening wet with saliva. Margot put her hand between her legs and felt the smooth slit there. Her pussy was soaked and she sat back and spread her legs so that Carly could see. She took her fingers, wet with cuntjuice, and rubbed the juice onto her pussylips until the whole area was shiny. Without any hair in the way, Carly got the full effect of drenched lips and the sweet slit that had provided the nectar. She breathed deeply and sucked the knob into her mouth.

"I'm wet," Margot said, "and I'm ready for it. Can I play with your toy?"

Carly moved back and indicated the rubber prick standing at attention. "Be my guest," she said.

Margot squatted over the dildo and used her fingers to spread her lips wide. The opening to her tunnel was clearly visible, hairless, waiting. Carly was bending down now, looking up at Margot from underneath so that she could see everything.

The plastic knob waited patiently. Margot moved down so that her pussylips were just touching it. Then she swung her hips back and forth, rubbing the whole length of her slit on the huge toy. A fine string of pussyjuice stretched from Margot's cunt to the knob as she did. Carly was transfixed. The juice on the head looked thick and creamy and had the lovely honey smell of Margot's cunt. Carly could almost imagine it slowly running down the shaft like a sweet liqueur.

Margot was achingly slow, prolonging both her own pleasure and Carly's, for both of them were enjoying this gorgeous woman atop the rubber pleasure-giver. The pink plastic was almost ruby against the stark creaminess of Margot's newly sheared mound. Her lips opened to accept the head and Margot paused with the tip right at the entrance to her tunnel. Then she moved ever so slightly, and the smooth head disappeared into the delicious crack.

Carly used her fingers to pull Margot's lips apart so that she could see her lover fill up with the dildo. Margot pushed herself down on it slowly, slowly, groaning as the rubber prick opened her to gain access. When all of the head was engulfed, she fucked it. It popped out, naked and shiny for just a moment, and then was taken back into that hot cave. It was an amazing sight. All of Margot's pussy spread to take it in, and then when the head was completely inside, the lips closed around the glans and held it firmly.

Now Margot took the device in deeper. She wanted to stay just on the head of it, teasing Carly with her shaved pussy, but it felt too good to have her cunt filled. She moved up and down on it, each time moving further down. The shaft, when she lifted herself up, was shiny with her juice.

Carly had an inspiration, and she got up, kissing Margot firmly before she left to go into the bathroom. When she came back, she had the hand mirror she had used to show Margot her new nakedness. Now she knelt on the floor in front of the rider and positioned the mirror so that Margot could see everything that was going on.

Margot was fascinated. Her shaved pussy looked delightful impaled on the dildo. Slowly she lifted herself up the whole length of the shaft. Her pussylips stretched down on it, as if trying to keep it inside. She played for a while with the head right at the entrance to her hole, then she sank down on it, watching the hairless lips fold inward to accept its massive width and length. Her groan was both for the sight of it and for the delicious fullness it produced.

"Now fuck it!" Carly said. One hand held the mirror, the other was among her bright red pubic hair, playing with her clit. "You love it, don't you? Show it! Fuck that prick hard!"

Margot couldn't do anything less. She was on fire now with her cunt so full. She had the dildo in completely and her ass was smacking against the cushion she was squatting on. She was riding it now. She discovered that in front of the dildo there was an area covered in soft, rubbery bumps. This was right where her clit came down and the bumps, like tiny fingers, massaged her sweetly distended button each time she slammed down on the dick. Each touch sent shivers through her.

Margot was fucking it as hard as she could now. Carly loved the sound of her asscheeks as they slapped against the rider. Margot's hair was flying wildly and her eyes were tightly closed. She was whispering, "Fuck me, fuck me, fuck me," like a chant, barely aware that she was doing it. Only one thing mattered to her now, and that was her enjoyment on this amazing device.

Carly, watching her, now had put the mirror down, and moved both hands between her legs. One was massaging her throbbing clit while the other was thrust firmly into her vagina, pushing in and out. The rhythm of her fingers in her cunt matched Margot's on the riding dildo. Not even touching, they were still fucking together.

Margot was bouncing on the device. Her tits moved with her and she reached down to take her nipples between her fingertips and squeeze them. She stretched them out, tweaking them, and groaned at the thrills she was giving herself. Her whole body was soaked with sex.

"Fuck it hard, Margot!" Carly whispered. She was giving it to herself just as hard with her fingers, and her other hand was almost pounding on her clit. Pushing it back and forth, up and down, she brought herself closer and closer to her goal.

"So hard!" Margot gasped in agreement. She was filled with the dildo and the rubber bumps were pounding on her clit. She had her tits stretched out, her fingers on her nipples and twisting them. Finally she felt as if she was at the crest of a great hill. She let herself go over the top of it, and fell long and deep into her orgasm.

When she saw Margot coming, Carly let herself go too. Hands working frantically in her cunt, she brought on her own climax, and side by side, the two rode out their peaks until both were spent.

Gasping, Margot slowed down and finally stopped. She was hunkered down on the rider, and the entire length of the thick shaft was still inside her steamy tunnel. By moving back and forth, she drained the last few shivers out and then slowly dismounted.

The shaft was soaked with her juice. With an almost overwhelming longing, Carly leaned over and licked it off. It was as rich and sweet as she had imagined. She couldn't stop until the whole device was clean. Then she kissed Margot deeply, who greedily sucked the taste of her own pussy from the tongue of her lover.

Somewhat shaky, they managed to get up to the daybed, where they collapsed beside each other.

Margot was still breathing hard and Carly was savoring the taste that lingered on her lips and tongue. She couldn't get enough of it.

Idly she ran her fingers over Margot's shorn pussy. The skin above her slit was so smooth it felt slippery even though it was dry. Her lips were still soaked, though, and Carly ran her finger over them and sucked the juice off, over and over, until the skin was clean. The gesture reminded Margot of someone cleaning a plate to get the last bit of chocolate sauce. For Carly, the thick nectar was just as sweet and just as desirable.

Once that was done, Carly's hand was replaced by Margot's own. Her shaved pussy felt so unusual and she just had to touch it. The skin seemed hotter than it ever had been, almost feverish, and as smooth as anything she could imagine. The cleft of her pussy and her lips felt so foreign without their hair and yet so familiar. She knew she would be reaching for it many times in the days to come, for it was so new and exciting.

"I've had my pussy shaved clean before," Carly said. "When it grows back it's going to itch like crazy."

"I kind of expected that," Margot said. Her fingers in her cunt were beginning to excite her again. "What's the best thing for it?"

Carly winked at her. "Shaving it again," she said. She had been so taken with the whole experience, she longed for the next time she could put out the razor and the mug carefully on the linen napkin and use the brush to whip up the thick cream to coat Margot's pussy again.

"I might just have to do that," Margot said. "How soon before I'll need another?"

"A week or so."

"And any volunteers?"

Carly laid back, closed her eyes and smiled. "Now what do you think?"

Chapter Twelve

Mistress of Mine

"In Matthew it says that no man can serve two masters," the tall, dark-haired woman said to me. "It does not necessarily refer to women."

That was immediately obvious. Here I was in front of two Mistresses, and even without being told, I knew that

I would be expected to fully serve them both. I was their submissive. Anything they told me to do would be done.

The dark-haired woman, Mistress Rachel, was the one I actually belonged to. She was, without a doubt, the most exciting person I had ever met and the most compelling dominatrix I had ever served.

This evening she was, as usual, stunning. Her clothing was made of patent leather that shone like glass, without a single spot on it anywhere. I knew that, because earlier in the week I had toiled for more than an hour making sure it was in the best of condition. It consisted of a bustier that accentuated my Mistress's breasts in a way that made me almost giddy, and a garter belt that left bare the sweet rich pussy that I was sometimes allowed to pleasure as a special treat. She also wore black stockings and tall black boots, patent leather with stiletto heels. I had cleaned those boots several times with shoe polish, and more than once with my tongue. I even remember the cut I sustained when I was ordered to suck the heel and I did not move quickly enough. My tongue was sore for weeks after that, but I learned never to disobey my Mistress when she gave me an order.

The other dominatrix was one I knew, although not very well. Mistress Astra was Mistress Rachel's good friend and I had sometimes seen her come into the house as I was leaving. She was someone I found it difficult to take my eyes away from. She was stunningly beautiful, in an unusual way that I did not often see. She had the white blonde hair of her Nordic ancestors and their light, pale coloring, but her hair was a huge mane that stretched down her back with a life of its own. Her eyes were steel blue and cold, her lips thin and pale. Even when she smiled, there was ice in it. I feared her almost as much as I feared my own Mistress.

She stood before me this evening in a costume as well. Hers was a red lace corset but the delicate designs of the lace, instead of softening the effect she had on me, seemed only to make her more domineering. It was a corset and I could see the tops of her large, soft breasts. Her pussy was also uncovered and the hair was so light it looked as if she had none there at all.

Of course I was only able to catch glimpses of both of them; I would have stared if I could have, but that would have rained cruel punishment down on me. My costume consisted only of a cold steel chain around my neck, the type a dog would wear, and cuffs on my wrists that were joined together behind my back. I was kneeling on the hardwood floor, which was not only achingly tough on my legs but was also cold. I had been ordered to this position by Mistress Rachel, who had then bound my wrists. Then she had been joined by Mistress Astra.

When Mistress Astra first came into the room, I didn't know what to think. To my surprise, I wasn't embarrassed to be seen by her, mostly because once I am under my Mistress's command, I am not permitted the luxury of pride. I did feel jealous, because I am fiercely possessive of my Mistress, a situation which I do not believe displeases her entirely. I did not want to share this session with another woman, but of course, that is not my decision to make. However, when Mistress Astra left and returned in the bright red costume with a riding crop in her hand, my jealousy gave way to intrigue. I had never served more than one Mistress at a time, and it seemed like a very exciting prospect to me.

Now I was in their hands, wondering what would happen to me. Although I dreaded some of the nastier punishments Mistress Rachel had given to me in the past, my cunt was nevertheless hot and wet. Kneeling, chained like an animal, I could smell the perfume of my own hot slit. My nipples were hard and tingling, aching for a touch I could not give to them. I longed for sexual relief but I knew it would not happen tonight. My personal pleasure was nothing. Everything was for the benefit of my Mistress.

While Mistress Astra ran one finger up and down the red leather riding crop she was carrying, my own Mistress Rachel carried a smaller, thicker leather whip, more suitable for training a dog. That, of course, was all I was to her, and to keep up the image she bent down and snapped a leather leash to the chain collar I was wearing.

"Now come along," she said, pulling on the leash. I tried to move forward on my knees, but it was impossible to keep my balance with my wrists tied behind my back, and after a few difficult motions I fell over on my side.

Of course, it was obvious that I had been set up. Within seconds, Mistress Astra was upon me. My buttocks were exposed to her when I was lying like that, and I hardly had time to realize what was happening when the crop came down across my ass. I yelped like a dog when it hit. My ass felt like a red-hot poker had been laid across the skin. Mistress Astra had considerable strength in her arms, and when she struck me twice more, I sobbed. My poor ass felt like it had been laid open.

"You're right, Rachel," Mistress Astra said to the dark-haired woman who held my leash. "Her skin really does come up a nice red."

"I told you it did," my Mistress smiled. "She can really take a lot, too. I think you'll find her quite to your liking."

Their words came to me muffled, for the blood was pounding in my ears and my eyes swam with tears. I really didn't enjoy the pain very much; unlike some submissives who reveled in it, I sometimes found it almost too much to take. What excited me was that I was in the complete control of a woman like Mistress Rachel and that I had to obey every command she gave me, no matter how difficult it was or even if it wasn't something I particularly wanted to do. Accepting pain from her was a duty that I fulfilled because it was my beloved Mistress who had given it to me.

"Poor little thing's too stupid to know that she can't walk with her hands tied," Mistress Rachel said. Her tone was condescending and I knew that I could only hold my tongue; if I were to say anything to defend myself, the riding crop would be sweet reward compared to the punishment I would receive. My Mistress bent down and released the snap ring that held my wrists together, although she did not remove the cuffs. I moved my arms slowly; they were very stiff from having been in such a position for so long.

Now I was allowed to walk behind them, on my hands and knees like an animal, led by the leash and collar. The hardwood floor pained my knees terribly, but I tried to ignore it. The two women paid me no more mind than if I were a well-trained dog out walking behind them on the street. I was led into another room, one that I knew all too well. I never failed to enter this particular room without a mixture of anticipation—for I would be allowed to serve my Mistress here—and dread, for instruments of terrible punishment were kept here and used to their fullest.

The room was set up specifically for domination. One wall contained rings screwed into the wall at all heights, from the floorboards right up to an inch from the ceiling. I had been attached to those topmost rings on several occasions, mostly by my wrists and once, in an excruciating position necessitating a ladder to get me there, by sturdy cuffs buckled around my ankles. That had been because I had dropped a glass I had been ordered to fill with wine. That was another error I went out of my way to avoid again.

There were a number of devices whose use might have puzzled most people, but when one is a dominatrix or a submissive, their use is immediately evident. One was a padded leather horse with rings on it that a submissive could straddle, or be pushed over, or spread out on, and either ordered to stay in place or chained to the rings. There was a table with rings on all sides so that a woman might be pushed down on it, bent at the waist, and secured in that most uncomfortable position. There was a wall covered with shelves, and upon them sat all manner of leather paddles, chains, cuffs, harnesses, gags, hoods, and other means of torture. There were also several soft, comfortable chairs upholstered in velvet. To the best of my knowledge, no submissive had ever sat upon them, and I doubted if any ever would.

My leash was snapped into one of the rings on the wall and I was left there, kneeling naked on the cold floor. Between two of the chairs was a small table containing a silver tray, two glasses, a bottle of wine. Jealously, I wondered if another submissive were in the house and had fetched it. I knew that Mistress Rachel had other women in her stable, and it bothered me to think of anyone else bringing pleasure to the woman I served.

The two women sat down in the chairs and Mistress Rachel poured wine for both of them. Then they ignored me, but that did not mean that I was left alone. Even though they did not look in my direction, I did not move a muscle. I had been ordered to stay there and stay there I would, even if the command to move was not given for several hours. I served my Mistress; that was what I did, and nothing would dissuade me from that.

They sipped at their wine. I had had nothing to drink for several hours, and my throat was dry. The sight of that wine made me even thirstier, but of course none was offered to me. Many years ago, when I first realized that I was a submissive and I found myself in the control of a Mistress, I learned quickly that nothing would be shared with me except commands and punishment. I also quickly learned that trying to avoid thirst by drinking a lot of water before I went to attend my Mistress was not the answer. Like food and drink, bathroom privileges were also given only at the Mistress's discretion, and at her discretion could be just as easily withheld. Sitting and suffering a full bladder was painful, but nothing compared to the consequences of not being able to hold it.

The two Mistresses were talking to each other quietly, about subjects in no way related to what they were doing. Sitting on chairs, sipping wine, wearing bustiers and corsets, their pussies uncovered, with a woman in chains a few feet away from them, they were discussing their accountants. Their lack of concern, surprisingly enough, excited me. I was so much in their control that they could ignore me, confident that I would remain right where I was until they turned their attention to me.

Then, in the middle of their conversation, Mistress Astra put one hand over the arm of her chair and between my Mistress's legs. Again I felt a bit jealous, but because this was another dominatrix, I forced myself to swallow such an emotion and just watch out of the corner of my eye.

My Mistress sank in her seat a little and opened her legs, so that Mistress Astra's long, pale fingers could reach all of her easily. I could imagine how good it might feel to have such fingers on my clit. My pussy was throbbing, for I would spend the entire session in a state of readiness that would not be fulfilled. I had to content myself with my excitement only and try not to think about blessed relief as I watched Mistress Rachel enjoy the touch of her friend's hand on her.

"I think," my Mistress said, "that we should try out the plan I discussed with you earlier."

"I would like that," Mistress Astra said, and bent over to kiss my Mistress slowly and seductively. Her voice was low and very suggestive and despite myself, I looked forward to receiving commands from her. I already had tasted her punishment, though, and I knew that I would be quick to obey anything she told me to do.

They put down their glasses and came over to me. I was cold inside, a reaction I always had whenever I realized that my Mistress had a plan for me. At the same time, my pussy was on fire and I looked forward to serving them both.

The leash was taken off my collar and I was allowed to stand up. I did this slowly, for my knees were very sore, and I was jabbed in the ribs by the short whip Mistress Rachel held to speed me up. I was ordered to move the two chairs, the table, and the serving set on it. I did this with difficulty, for the chairs were heavy, and I was hurried along by both Mistresses. My Mistress Rachel gave me a shove across the shoulders with her short whip when I moved the first chair, and Mistress Astra cruelly sliced the riding crop across the backs of my thighs when I struggled with the second one. The table was simple to move, but I was very careful when I took the tray, the bottle of wine and the two glasses across the room. The glasses still had wine in them and I knew that spilling even a drop would be disaster.

When I finished, Mistress Rachel took my collar in her hand and I had to follow her over to the table. My heart sank. The table was cruel punishment, for it meant bending at the waist and leaning forward. When the chains are finally released and the submissive is ordered to stand up straight, the muscles of the back feel as if they have been torn in half. It takes days to recover from this particular device.

Of course my concern about my well-being meant nothing to either of them. They were Mistresses, I was a submissive, and I would do as they said. I did, bending over the table. It was cold and I set my upper body down on it gingerly. Mistress Rachel, unhappy about my reluctance, pushed me down hard with the whip across my shoulders. I then received two blows across my already bruised asscheeks for being so slow.

My hands were chained to rings on the sides of the table, so that I lay with my arms stretched out from my body. Mistress Rachel went across to the well-stocked shelves, and when she returned, I felt her strong fingers buckle heavy cuffs around my ankles. These, in turn, were attached to rings on the table legs. My own legs were now spread wide apart, so far that my thighs quickly began to ache where they met my crotch. I prayed that the soothing numbness would come soon.

I was surprised that I was not blindfolded, for Mistress Rachel generally covered my eyes when I was on the table. Instead I had a very clear view of the two chairs. I wondered what was in store for me, for when they sat down they did not order me to avert my eyes. I was allowed to stare at them, which I did. Even bound as I was, I was fascinated by them.

I then saw that my Mistress had a vibrator. It was a fairly large one, pink in color, smooth at the tip. "I put new batteries in it this morning," she said to Mistress Astra, who nodded. "I don't want it to run out just when we need it."

So saying, she turned it on. It had a dial at one end of it, and she set it at its lowest setting. In the quiet room, its buzzing sounded very loud.

My Mistress spread her legs apart and I was treated to the sight of her smooth thighs above the stocking tops and the warm, dark pussy in between. My mouth watered at the sight and I hoped that I would be given permission to finish any job the vibrator started. I was often ordered to pleasure her, to put my tongue in there and lap at her, but of course it was never enough for me. I could have stayed down there for hours and still not be satisfied.

Mistress Astra reached over and slipped a hand inside the patent leather bustier so that she could feel my Mistress's nipples. My Mistress rubbed the vibrator over that wet delight between her legs, and suddenly I realized that my own tongue was sticking out, wanting to touch.

My Mistress noticed and laughed at me. "See, Astra, they're just like animals," she said, and the blonde-haired woman laughed also. "Just like Pavlov's dog. You show them a pussy and see what they do."

Their laughter subsided as Mistress Rachel rubbed the vibrator harder on her pussy. Gradually she turned the dial, so that the vibrator buzzed even more.

"Now?" Mistress Astra asked. "I think so," my Mistress said. "She looks hot enough." Mistress Astra got up, picking up the riding crop and holding it with one hand. In her other hand, I saw that she, too, had a vibrator. It was a white one, very plain, with a dial on the end of it as well. I thought she was going to apply it to her own pussy, but instead, she went behind me. Tied to the table as I was, I could see only my Mistress in her chair, the pink vibrator between her cuntlips. Only the sound of Mistress Astra's impossibly high heels on the wooden floor told me where she was.

I jumped when I felt the touch of her hand on my thighs. It was a kind touch, very soothing, but instead of putting me at ease, it started my heart pounding and I began to breathe rapidly. I was frightened. I knew that kindness from any Mistress was just a setup for cruelty to come, and I did not know at what point her cool fingers would be replaced by the nasty riding crop.

Her hand moved up toward my pussy. "What does it look like?" Mistress Rachel asked, the vibrator buzzing between her legs.

"It's all wet," Mistress Astra replied. "How disgusting. It would be nice if they could come up with a slave that didn't do such a thing."

"It would," my Mistress said, and put her head back as she turned the vibrator up another notch. The plastic tip was wet with her juice. I desperately wanted to suck it off and taste it on my tongue.

Then I heard the vibrator buzzing behind me, and moments later, Mistress Astra applied it to my pussy. I groaned out loud, involuntarily, and only afterwards realized that I might be punished for it. I was not. It was obvious that both Mistresses had expected me to do it, even wanted me to.

The vibrator felt delicious on my hot, throbbing pussy and despite myself, I squirmed in my bonds, trying to move my most needy clit to touch it. Mistress Astra knew what I was doing, and she kept it away. When my breathing became hard, she took the vibrator off me, and only when I had relaxed did she apply it again. Once again my body jumped. It felt so good, so novel. I had never been allowed such delightful relief from a Mistress before.

Perhaps my excitement was why I did not question their motives. I only thought that finally I would be allowed to come and to relieve the almost overwhelming pressure that tightened in my belly and spilled over into the wetness of my cunt. I kept my eyes on my Mistress, who was now rubbing the vibrator up and down the lips of her pussy, glistening with her juice. I felt a oneness with her I had never felt before. For the first time we were experiencing the same thing at the same time. Surely no submissive in history was as lucky as I!

I was now gasping, trembling in my bonds. The vibrator on my pussy was sensational and I was so close to coming I could taste it. I was at the peak, trying to urge myself over it, wanting desperately to spill over into the bliss of the other side. So close, so close, so close...

Smack! In one swift motion, so quick I could not even follow it, Mistress Astra pulled the vibrator away and brought the crop down on my ass. I screamed. The crop came down three more times, leaving white-hot stripes across my flesh. I screamed again and begged for mercy.

The blonde-haired dominatrix came around to the front of the table; my Mistress Rachel was still sitting with the vibrator between her legs. "Foolish scum slave," Mistress Astra said, as she put the riding crop to my face. "Kiss it now." I did.

"Did you honestly believe that you would be allowed to come?" she continued, as she moved to sit down in her chair. "All of you are far more stupid than we could possibly imagine. Of course, that is what makes you so amusing." She smiled at me, as cold as any grin I had ever seen, and then she leaned over and kissed my Mistress hard and deep. With the buzzing vibrator between her legs and Mistress Astra's tongue in her mouth, my Mistress Rachel gave herself over and came.

It was now Mistress Astra's turn, and the wet vibrator was handed over to her. My Mistress's juice on the plastic made it slippery and it slid easily over the white-haired pussy.

It was now my Mistress Rachel's turn to take up the white vibrator—a special one procured just for me, for never would they allow their pink device to be polluted by the pussy of a slave—and to stand behind me. It was a very difficult punishment for me. I knew exactly what was going to happen, and I knew that if I were to remain there, my back aching and my thighs sore from being spread so wide, and enjoy the touch of the vibrator upon me, it would be especially painful when the device was taken away and the whip substituted. I was determined to keep my mind elsewhere, to think of anything except that tip on my sodden clit, so that I would not be trapped again.

Of course that was impossible. Mistress Astra smiled coldly at me again and rubbed the vibrator between her legs. It was pointless closing my eyes for I knew they would be forced open. She licked one finger and pointedly used it to rub her clit, making sure that I saw her satisfied expression and the way her button moved under her fingertip. I was hot again and when Mistress Rachel touched the vibrator to my pussy, there was no chance of concentrating on anything else. Once again I was swept into the vortex, toward the peak, hoping against hope that this time I would be permitted to come.

Like a fool I almost believed it, which is why the whip across the small of my back was such a shock. Mistress Astra came just at the moment that the vibrator was taken from me and the leather whip applied. Her ecstasy and my agony met across the room. She increased her pleasure with my pain, and my suffering was only magnified watching her enjoy her orgasm.

They sat down again in front of me and finished the wine. Mistress Rachel knew I was thirsty and at one point, she got up and wetted one finger with the golden liquid, then thrust it between my lips. I sucked on it desperately. But the alcohol in it, and the small quantity I was given, only increased my thirst. Stiff, striped with lashes, bound and aching, I could only watch these two as they sat on their comfortable chairs and finished their drinks.

The session was over; they stood up and put their

glasses down. I was given three more blows across my shoulders, and then the clips were unsnapped and I was free. When I tried to stand I fell; my stiff limbs would not support me. I was told to stay there and not to move until they left the room.

"When we leave," Mistress Rachel said to me, "you may take off your bindings. Your clothes are in the hall by the door. You will not disturb us when you go."

"No, Mistress," I whispered. My arms and legs, no longer held firmly in place, burned as the feeling came back into them. It was like being held in a fire, and I had to bite my lip to keep from crying out.

They walked out of the room, the sight of them walking away in those delicious costumes and those stiletto heels remaining with me for quite a while. Then, slowly, with fingers that did not want to respond, I unbuckled the cuffs from my wrists and ankles. It was difficult to stand and even harder to walk, but eventually I made my way over to the shelves and put the cuffs back in their proper place. Even as I did it, I knew that Mistress Rachel would tell me they had been put back incorrectly at our next session. Looking over the collection of whips, paddles, nine-tails, and latex hoods, I wondered which of them would be used to confirm this.

I put my hands behind my neck to release the chain collar. When my fingers found the clasp, my whole body went icy cold. It was closed with its ring, but unknown to me, Mistress Rachel had also snapped a tiny padlock on it. I had wondered what the sound was when she had done it up, but hadn't thought much of it at the time. Now, desperately, I searched the shelves for the key. I could find nothing.

I could hear a muffled chime and I knew it was the grandfather clock that sat in the hallway. I had to hurry, for if I took too long to dress and leave I would be severely punished for my tardiness. I realized that the lack of a key was not an oversight on my Mistress's part.

I did not know when I would be next called to serve her; it could be tomorrow, it could be a month from now, depending on her whim. I would not be able to open the padlock until then. It was summertime and a high-collared shirt would be very uncomfortable, but it would not do to go to work with a dog's collar visible about my throat. I would just have to find a way to hide it.

At least until the next time I would kneel on the floor, naked, under the command of the Mistress I adored. Then I would wear it openly and proudly as a badge of my servitude to this woman. For now, it would be a secret that would be hidden from the rest of the world, a secret which I would carry close to me. I was my Mistress's submissive. There was nothing else that mattered.

Chapter Thirteen

Bed and Breakfast

The young man with the tight-fitting jeans came out from the garage, wiping his greasy hands on a rag that was stiff with dirt.

Charlotte and Robin stayed where they were, sitting on the uncomfortable seats in the waiting room. The young man came up to the counter, expecting them to jump up and come over as most customers did. Instead, the two gorgeous women watched him, waiting for him to come to them. After pausing a moment behind the counter, he did.

"Well, ma'am," he began, "it's just what I thought it was. Your fuel pump is shot. You need a new one."

"Then put one on," Charlotte said, a little exasperated. She was already unhappy about leaving Liz behind in her cottage in Provincetown, and now here they were stranded on a small highway in a town so small it was barely a spot on the map.

About two hours after they left, the car had started acting up, bucking and stalling; fortunately she had been able to get it this far. The garage was small but it was the only one in town.

"That's the problem, ma'am," the mechanic continued. "I don't have one in stock and the parts store's closed now. They won't be open until nine tomorrow morning."

"Wonderful," Charlotte said sarcastically. "You can't give us a temporary repair to get us home?"

"No, ma'am," the mechanic said. "They're all electronic now. They either work or they don't. I'm sorry, ma'am, but your car won't be finished until tomorrow."

Charlotte and Robin looked at each other. Why couldn't this have happened in Provincetown, where they could have used it as an excuse to extend their week with Liz? "I don't suppose there's a hotel in town, is there?" Robin asked.

"No, ma'am," the mechanic said. "But there is a bed

and breakfast just a few miles from here. I can call them if you like. Miss Lydia can come out and pick you up."

"That will be fine," Charlotte said, and she waited while the young man went back into an office and picked up the phone.

"Well, I suppose it could be worse," Robin said. "At least we were able to get this far."

"Yes, but a bed and breakfast?" Charlotte moaned. "I don't like staying in someone's house. It's probably some little basement apartment with a hard bed and skimpy little towels. They'll probably look at us really funny when we tell them we want one room together. And the food—it'll probably be cold, greasy eggs and bacon and bad coffee for breakfast. What I wouldn't give for the Ritz-Carlton to be next door!"

Her gloomy expression continued as the young man came back into the room. "Miss Lydia is coming out right now," he said. "Do you have bags in the trunk? I can get them out for you if you like."

"Please do," Charlotte said, and she turned and looked out at the small road that stretched out in front of the garage. Liz had recommended it, saying that the scenery was worth the extra miles and the slower speed limits. It was a beautiful drive, it was true, but Liz was going to pay for this! Charlotte West, connoisseur of the finest hotels and the best restaurants in the country, staying in a bed and breakfast. Just wait until she found a telephone to call her friend, undoubtedly sitting right now on her porch sipping a glass of wine!

Some twenty minutes later, a minivan pulled up to the door. It was almost brand new, spotless, with

"Pineapple Acres" written in graceful script on the front doors along with a stylized picture of the fruit. A woman about Charlotte's age got out and met them.

"I'm Lydia Wallace," she said, and shook hands with both of them. She was very good looking, her brown hair streaked appealingly with blonde. Her snug blue jeans, her tailored plaid shirt, and gold-rimmed glasses were at once informal and stylish. "I'm sorry we have to meet under these circumstances, but I think you'll enjoy your stay with us." Charlotte and Robin could detect the hint of a Southern accent in her voice.

"I was looking forward to getting home tonight," Charlotte said. She was still somewhat sullen.

"Well, Dave's a very good mechanic," Lydia said as she opened the van's sliding door and put their bags inside. "If he says your car will be ready tomorrow, it will be." She held the door open and waited for both of them to sit inside.

Robin, who was taking the situation much better, began chatting with their driver. "Why 'Pineapple Acres'?" she asked. "Obviously that isn't what you grow in the back forty."

Lydia laughed; it was a charming sound. "No, you're right there," she said. "I'm originally from South Carolina, and in the South, the pineapple is the symbol of hospitality. At our inn, that's the most important thing."

"You said it's 'our' inn," Robin said. "Do you run it with your husband?"

"No," Lydia said, after a slight pause. "My partner is Meg Aldsworth. The house was her grandfather's and we've been running it as an inn for twelve years now."

She turned off the road and went up a long driveway. The house was stunning, and Charlotte forgot her gloom as she admired it. It was very old and ornate, decorated with the gingerbread trim so popular at the turn of the century. The light brick of the house blended perfectly with the wooden trim painted gold. The gardens around the house were unbelievably lush, a rainbow of colors that moved as the flower heads swayed in the breeze. A sign out front was decorated with a pineapple, as were the posts on the porch. The porch itself went right around the house and was filled with chairs and a swing that hung from the porch roof.

"It's beautiful," Charlotte breathed as the van came to a halt out front and Lydia opened the door for them. "Certainly not what I'd been expecting."

They went inside. A woman came in from the kitchen, wearing an apron, her hands dusty with flour. She was shorter than Lydia, her hair long and black, her smile almost infectious. She wiped her hands on her apron before she greeted the guests. "Dave told us you would be coming," she said. "I figured you hadn't had any dinner yet."

"No, we haven't," Charlotte admitted.

"Then Lydia can show you to your rooms, and I'll put the biscuits in the oven," the woman said. Like Lydia, her voice gave away her Southern origins. "Don't be too long, though. The guests wait for the biscuits, not the other way around."

The two women followed Lydia through the house. Charlotte's preconceptions came crashing down as she looked about. The rooms were finished in mahogany trim and the floors, scrubbed to a high gloss, were decorated with hand-woven rugs. The paintings on the walls were oils, the furniture antique and well preserved. Oak stairs led up to the bedrooms. On the landing the window was outlined in stained glass, and the last of the day's sunlight filtered through and left colorful patterns on the floor.

"Here is your room," Lydia said to Charlotte, as she opened the door. Charlotte looked inside. It was as beautifully done as her own, with a large bed, starched white curtains, thick carpets.

"It's very nice," Charlotte said. "But if you don't mind, we'd rather share a room."

Both she and Robin were expecting an argument, but to their surprise, Lydia seemed to brighten up. "Of course," she said. "Then you don't want that one, it's too small. Come down here."

"But that room's huge," Robin said.

"Oh, these old houses have caverns, not rooms," Lydia smiled. "That one's a closet compared to our master bedroom."

She was right. The room she led them to ran almost the width of the entire house. The bed was king-sized, with six pillows and a feather duvet arranged over it. Late summer flowers, taken from the garden, spilled out of a vase on the huge mahogany dresser. One wall was almost completely made of windows. Lydia showed them the bathroom, luxuriously finished, and the walk-in closet. "This late in the season everything slows down," she said. "You're the only guests we have tonight, so don't worry about disturbing anyone else. If you want to have a shower at 2 A.M., go right ahead."

She put their bags on the cedar chest at the foot of the bed. "You'll probably want to freshen up," she said. "I'll come back upstairs and call you when dinner's ready. It will be about half an hour. Oh, there's a brochure on the table. You might want to look it over and see what our inn is all about." Then she turned and left.

Charlotte looked out the window; there were no other houses nearby and the path stretched down into a garden that seemed to have no end. How wrong she had been! This old house was as fine as any hotel she had stayed in.

Robin, meanwhile, sat down on the bed and picked up the brochure. She looked through it, turned it over and then let out a whoop. "Charlotte, come look at this!" she said.

Charlotte did. The brochure was filled with pictures of the grounds and the rooms, and on the back was a photo of Lydia and Meg together. The inn's address and phone number was printed on the bottom. Just below it, so small that it was almost unnoticeable, was a pink triangle.

"I thought so!" Robin crowed. "No wonder she didn't bat an eyelash when we asked for one room. They share one themselves."

"Isn't that great," Charlotte agreed. "Well, we sure have a welcome mat set out here."

"I'm going to have a shower," Robin said. "I feel dusty. Are you in or out?"

"Maybe later," Charlotte said, and she stretched out

on the bed, enjoying its softness and the fluffiness of the pillows.

Robin went into the bathroom. It was beautifully decorated and the towels were thick; the shower stall was large and spotless. She undressed, admiring her body in the full-length mirror on the wall. Then she stepped into the shower, closed the glass door behind her, and turned on the water. She loved hot showers and the temperature and pressure were perfect. She stood under the stream for a long time and then reached for the soap.

Her eyes closed under the showerhead, she heard the glass door open and close. "I was lying there thinking about you," Charlotte said. "I couldn't let you stay in here alone."

Robin turned and they embraced and kissed deeply. The water ran hot and sweet over both of them. Then their hands moved down, to touch pussies wet from both water and their own need.

Charlotte's hand found the soap. It was a big bath bar, delicately scented, and she stood back and used it to soap Robin all over. She started at her throat, running her hands and the soap over the smooth dark skin, and then moved down to her breasts. She loved the way her hands slid over the skin effortlessly.

Robin groaned as Charlotte's fingers washed her nipples thoroughly. Then the soap went down her belly and found the place between her legs.

She gasped as Charlotte used the corner of the soap to press the wet lips apart. It was an unusual feeling, for the soap slid across her clit and still awakened the hot thrills in her. Now Charlotte's other hand was there as well, slipping a water-soaked finger into the heat of her tunnel. The smooth tight walls were hotter than the water that poured down over both of them.

Robin now had her legs open wide and Charlotte was moving the bar of soap quickly on her crotch. It pushed her clit back and forth the way she loved, and soon she was gasping and moaning. Wet all over, hot from both the water and the hands in her cunt, Robin cried out. Her orgasm caught her completely by surprise, it was so fast and intense. When it was finished she was almost dizzy.

"What's that?" Charlotte said, and she opened the shower door slightly. She could hear Lydia knocking at their bedroom door, reminding them that dinner would be ready shortly. She called out to say they would be finished and downstairs soon.

"Like I'm in any shape to move fast," Robin moaned. Her whole body was still loose and relaxed from her orgasm.

"Well, you're half washed now," Charlotte said, and spun her lover around so that she could soap her back. When they finished, they quickly dressed in loose, informal cotton pants and shirts that they had bought in Provincetown.

The large pine table in the dining room was set for two. "Aren't you eating?" Robin asked.

"Well, we don't generally eat with the guests," Lydia said. "We have a table in the kitchen."

"Nonsense," Charlotte said. "We'd be offended if you didn't eat with us." Their host smiled and hurried to bring in the extra place settings.

Once again Charlotte's misgivings were unfounded. The greasy, poor meal she'd expected turned out to be a Southern delight. There were thick slices of ham with red-eye gravy, beans cooked with lemon and almonds, candied sweet potatoes and, of course, the biscuits, hot and fluffy. They were so good that Charlotte ate far more than she thought she could, and when they were gone, along with a slice of pecan pie that she just couldn't turn down, she said that she'd need a walk before bed. Lydia pointed the two of them to the garden. The path was long and winding and it was dark before they realized it; when they got back to the house they were both so tired that they said their good-nights, went upstairs, and tucked themselves under the feather comforter with only a good-night kiss shared between them. They were asleep within minutes.

Robin woke first, to the dawn light coming in through the huge windows. She looked at her watch; it was only five thirty. She snuggled in beside Charlotte, who mumbled in her sleep but did not wake up.

Her eyes opened at a sound she could not identify. At first she thought it might be birds, or a cat meowing, but even though she listened intently it didn't seem to be either one.

Curious, she slipped out of bed and put on her robe. The sound was still audible and she opened the bedroom door. It was coming from down the hall.

Charlotte, aware that she was now alone in the bed, opened her eyes and sat up. "What is it?" she whispered.

"Listen!" Robin whispered back. Charlotte turned her head and listened for a moment.

"What is it?"

"I don't know," Robin said. "I'm going to go see."

"Maybe it's just Lydia or Meg in the kitchen," Charlotte said, as she sank back into the pillow.

"I don't think so," Robin whispered. "It's down the hall." She opened the bedroom door completely and then turned at another sound. Charlotte was out of bed, putting on her own robe.

The two of them walked down the long hallway. All of the doors to the various rooms were open, but the sound seemed to be coming from the end one. It was the bedroom Lydia had first offered to them. Gingerly, Charlotte and Robin stopped at the doorway and peeked inside. They could hardly believe their eyes.

Lydia and Meg were on the large bed, both of them naked. Meg was lying on the bottom and Lydia was over her in the sixty-nine position and each had her tongue in the other's cunt, licking wildly. The sound Robin had heard was their moaning. The women were oblivious to them, interested only in the pussy they were licking.

Charlotte and Robin were rooted to the spot, unable to look away. Lydia became aware of them first. She stopped instantly and got up; Meg stared also. Both of them had faces as red as fire. Suddenly Charlotte and Robin were just as embarrassed for having stared.

"I'm so sorry," Lydia said, looking for something to cover herself up with. "We should've closed the door."

"We shouldn't have stood here staring," Robin began, but for some reason she could not pull herself away. Meg, more in control of the situation, laughed.

"Well then," she said, "why don't the two of you just come in here?"

It was as if the spell had been broken. Lydia, bolstered by her lover's words, got up and brought her guests into the room. She stood before Robin and slowly untied the belt that held her robe together. Charlotte was drawn to Meg, who stayed on the bed, pulled her down, and kissed her hard.

"Sixty-nine is my favorite number," Meg sighed, and Charlotte took the hint right away. She also dropped her robe and Meg stretched on the bed, waiting, admiring Charlotte's delicious body. Charlotte was so hot she didn't even spend time sucking on Meg's nipples, even though they were pointed and hard. She arranged herself on top of the prone woman and immediately starting licking.

Robin and Lydia, meanwhile, were in each other's arms, kissing deeply. When they saw Meg and Charlotte going at each other, they also moved toward the bed. Within moments they were also on it, Robin on the bottom and Lydia on top, licking and sucking.

Charlotte was completely taken with the whole scene. Here they were, with each other's partners, sharing a bed and eating pussy for all they were worth. Their own moans were exciting but the moans of their partners beside them sent them right off.

Lydia was completely taken with it all. She had never had a black partner before and the racial contrast excited her. She loved the sight of Robin's ruby red pussy and the smoothness and richness of her dark skin. Several times she stopped licking and used her hands to caress Robin's clit, staring at the sweet lips and the large knot of flesh that she was pleasuring. The taste was delicious on her lips and before long she had to put her tongue back into that well. The juice was a drink that she had to consume.

Robin, meanwhile, was thoroughly enjoying Lydia's weight on her and the pussy that was being ground into her mouth. She couldn't lick fast enough. All four of them, rather than taking their time and enjoying a long session, were going like crazy. The circumstances, the immediate invitation, the speed with which new tongue met new pussy did not call for romanticism. This was raw sex, a raw need. Drawn-out courtships could wait until later.

Meg was using both her tongue and her hands now. Her fingers were in Charlotte's pussy while her mouth was firmly on the swollen button. Charlotte gasped and licked her finger to wet it, then used it to tease the entrance to Meg's ass. This was obviously something Meg adored, for she squealed and pressed even closer, trying to push herself onto the finger that impaled her. Charlotte inserted it deeper and was rewarded by Meg sucking on her clit. When her finger was in as far as it would go, right to the knuckle, Meg sighed happily and continued her dance on Charlotte's cunt.

With everyone working so feverishly, it could not last forever. Robin was the first to come, and Meg used her fingers to bring it on so that she had the pleasure of seeing Robin's cunt twitch and shudder with the spasms. She herself came only moments later, and she cried out and pushed her pussy down on Robin as hard as she could, until it was all over.

Meg was beginning to squirm in a way that Char-lotte identified easily, and she could feel the muscles of Meg's tight rosebud grasping her finger even as her mouth filled with the delicious fluid from Meg's cunt. Charlotte was very close herself, and she held it off until Meg began to tremble. At that point she concentrated completely on her clit, lashed by Meg's tongue. As soon as Meg started to come, Charlotte reached her own climax, and together the two of them shared this hottest union.

All four were shy again when they separated, lying beside each other on the bed. Fortunately it passed quickly and as the morning light streamed through the window they were discussing what they had done. Robin and Charlotte felt like they had finally come home.

Meg, ever the gracious hostess, finally got up and tied her robe about herself, then left for the kitchen despite protests that breakfast could wait. "I'm not lying here any longer without a coffee in me," she laughed, and when the other three thought about steaming mugs taken out on the front porch, watching the flowers open in the sun's light after the cool night, they laughingly told her to hurry up.

A true Southerner, Meg finally came out of the kitchen not only with fresh coffee, but also with a pan of cornbread, perfectly fried eggs, and sausage patties for all of them. They sat on the porch, all of them in their robes, like friends who had known each other all their lives.

They were just finishing up when the phone rang; Lydia hurried inside to answer it. After a few minutes, she came back out.

"It's Dave down at the garage," she said. "He's really sorry, but the local supplier doesn't have a fuel pump to fit your car. It has to come from the city and it will take three hours longer than he expected. He hopes you aren't angry."

Charlotte looked out at the expanse of gardens, at the three women in their robes with nothing underneath, and she took a long swallow of her coffee before she answered. "Tell him," she said, "to take his time."

Chapter Fourteen

Nunc Est Bibendum

It was less than a minute to midnight, and all eyes were on the television. The ball began its slow descent, and the countdown was on. We all counted with it. When the ball finally reached the bottom and the crowd in Times Square went wild, so did we:

Noisemakers were spun and blown, and Carly had an old pot she banged with a wooden spoon.

Then it was time for kisses all around, some quick and friendly, some long and lingering, deep as any kiss could be. When it had finally died down, Rachel handed me the bottle of champagne that had been sitting in the ice bucket waiting.

I wrapped the bottle in a napkin and worked at the cork, praying that it would not break off in the neck. I didn't know why I worried so much; in ten years it had never happened. This year was no exception. It came out cleanly, with a golden wisp following it. I didn't realize everyone had been holding their breath until they all exhaled at the same time.

The glasses were filled and passed out. As I did every year, I stood and made the toast.

"It has certainly been quite a year," I said. "A lot has happened since we got together last year."

I went around the room, toasting each one in turn. Charlotte and Robin were together as always, sitting close on the sofa, hands held tightly. Rachel was stunningly beautiful as always, and Astra was smiling as she held her glass, ready to drink. Carly was outrageous as always, her hair colored bright orange and a new gold ring through her nose. Margot sat in a chair beside her and looked over at her frequently.

"There is a special toast this year," I continued, turning to the couple sharing the loveseat. "To Nora Stevens, who was our newest member last year. Nora, did you buy the champagne and put it away like I told you?"

"I certainly did," Nora smiled, squeezing the hand of the woman beside her.

"Then, Kate Silvers, this year it is your turn to buy a bottle of good champagne and put it away," I said to the red-haired woman sitting beside Nora. "Welcome to our circle of friends. And a toast to Nora and Kate, our newest couple. May you be happy forever."

At that, the glasses were raised, clinked together, and the sparkling wine was sipped.

I looked around at all of them. We were a circle of friends, it was true, but more than that we were a family. We interacted with each other, we loved each other, we depended on each other. I felt warm inside just being with all of them.

Then I looked across the room, and my eyes met Rachel's. She was smiling ever so slightly, and I must have raised one eyebrow in a question. Subtly, she nodded, and my pussy almost flooded right there. "*To auld lang syne,*" I said, and held up my glass to her. "Indeed," she said. And then both of us sat, waiting patiently. It was a whole new year, and anything could happen.

NOW AVAILABLE

The Blue Moon Erotic Reader IV

A testimonial to the publication of quality erotica, *The Blue Moon Erotic Reader IV* presents more than twenty romantic and exciting excerpts from selections spanning a variety of periods and themes. This is a historical compilation that combines generous extracts from the finest forbidden books with the most extravagant samplings that the modern erotica imagination has created. The result is a collection that is provocative, entertaining, and perhaps even enlightening. It encompasses memorable scenes of youthful initiations into the mysteries of sex, notorious confessions, and scandalous adventures of the powerful, wealthy, and notable. From the classic erotica of *Wanton Women*, and *The Intimate Memoirs of an Edwardian Dandy* to modern tales like Michael Hemmingson's *The Rooms*, good taste, passion, and an exalted desire are abound, making for a union of sex and sensibility that is available only once in a Blue Moon.

With selections by Don Winslow, Ray Gordon, M. S. Valentine, P. N. Dedeaux, Rupert Mountjoy, Eve Howard, Lisabet Sarai, Michael Hemmingson, and many others.

The Best of the Erotic Reader

"The Erotic Reader series offers an unequaled selection of the hottest scenes drawn from the finest erotic writing." — *Elle*

This historical compilation contains generous extracts from the world's finest forbidden books including excerpts from *Memories of a Young Don Juan*, *My Secret Life*, *Autobiography of a Flea*, *The Romance of Lust*, *The Three Chums*, and many others. They are gathered together here to entertain, and perhaps even enlighten. From secret texts to the scandalous adventures of famous people, from youthful initiations into the mysteries of sex to the most notorious of all confessions, *Best of the Erotic Reader* is a stirring complement to the senses. Containing the most evocative pieces covering several eras of erotic fiction, *Best of the Erotic Reader* collects the most scintillating tales from the seven volumes of *The Erotic Reader*. This comprehensive volume is sure to include delights for any taste and guaranteed to titillate, amuse, and arouse the interests of even the most veteran erotica reader.

NOW AVAILABLE

Color of Pain, Shade of Pleasure
Edited by Cecilia Tan

In these twenty-one tales from two out-of-print classics, *Fetish Fantastic* and *S/M Futures*, some of today's most unflinching erotic fantasists turn their futuristic visions to the extreme underground, transforming the modern fetishes of S/M, bondage, and eroticized power exchange into the templates for new sexual worlds. From the near future of S/M in cyberspace, to a future police state where the real power lies in manipulating authority, these tales are from the edge of both sexual and science fiction.

The Governess
M. S. Valentine

Lovely Miss Hunnicut eagerly embarks upon a career as a governess, hoping to escape the memories of her broken engagement. Little does she know that Crawleigh Manor is far from the respectable household it appears to be. Mr. Crawleigh, in particular, devotes himself to Miss Hunnicut's thorough defiling. Soon the young governess proves herself worthy of the perverse master of the house—though there may be even more depraved powers at work in gloomy Crawleigh Manor . . .

Claire's Uptown Girls
Don Winslow

In this revised and expanded edition, Don Winslow introduces us to Claire's girls, the most exclusive and glamorous escorts in the world. Solicited by upper-class Park Avenue businessmen, Claire's girls have the style, glamour and beauty to charm any man. Graced with supermodel beauty, a meticulously crafted look, and a willingness to fulfill any man's most intimate dream, these girls are sure to fulfill any man's most lavish and extravagant fantasy.

Don Winslow's Victorian Erotica
Don Winslow

The English manor house has long been a place apart; a place of elegant living where, in splendid isolation the gentry could freely indulge their passions for the outdoor sports of riding and hunting. Of course, there were those whose passions ran towards "indoor sports"—lascivious activities enthusiastically, if discreetly, pursued by lusty men and sensual women behind large and imposing stone walls of baronial splendor, where they were safely hidden from prying eyes. These are tales of such licentious decadence from behind the walls of those stately houses of a bygone era.

The Garden of Love
Michael Hemmingson

Three Erotic Thrillers from the Master of the Genre

In The *Comfort of Women*, the oddly passive Nicky Bayless undergoes a sexual re-education at the hands (and not only the hands) of a parade of desperate women who both lead and follow him through an underworld of erotic extremity. The narrator of *The Dress* is troubled by a simple object that may have supernatural properties. "My wife changed when she wore The Dress; she was the Ashley who came to being a few months ago. She was the wife I preferred, and I worried about that. I understood that The Dress was, indeed, an entity all its own, with its own agenda, and it was possessing my wife." In *Drama,* playwright Jonathan falls into an affair with actress Karen after the collapse of his relationship with director Kristine. But Karen's free-fall into debauchery threatens to destroy them both.

The ABZ of Pain and Pleasure
Edited by A. M. LeDeluge

A true alphabet of the unusual, *The ABZ of Pain and Pleasure* offers the reader an understanding of the language of the lash. Beginning with Aida and culminating with Zanetti, this book offers the amateur and adept a broad acquaintance with the heroes and heroines of this unique form of sexual entertainment. The Marquis de Sade is represented here, as are Jean de Berg (author of *The Image*), Pauline Réage (author of *The Story of O* and *Return to the Château*), P. N. Dedeaux (author of *The Tutor* and *The Prefect*), and twenty-two others.

NOW AVAILABLE

Folies D'Amour
Anne-Marie Villefranche

From the international best-selling pen of Anne-Marie Villefranche comes another 'improper' novel about the affairs of an intimate circle of friends and lovers. In the stylish Paris of the 1920s, games of love are played with reckless abandon. From the back streets of Montmartre to the opulent hotels on the Rue de Rivoli, the City of Light casts an erotic spell.

The Best of Ironwood
Don Winslow

Ostensibly a finishing school for young ladies, Ironwood is actually that singular institution where submissive young beauties are rigorously trained in the many arts of love. For James, our young narrator, Ironwood is a world where discipline knows few boundaries. This collection gathers the very best selections from the Ironwood series and reveals the essence of the Ironwood woman—a consummate blend of sexuality and innocence.

The Uninhibited
Ray Gordon

Donna Ryan works in a research laboratory where her boss has developed a new hormone treatment with some astounding and unsuspected side effects. Any woman who comes into contact with the treatment finds her sexual urges so dramatically increased that she loses all her inhibitions. Donna accidentally picks up one of the patches and finds her previously suppressed cravings erupting in an ecstatic orgy of liberated impulses. What ensues is a breakthrough to thrilling dimensions of wild, unrestrained sexuality.

Blue Angel Nights
Margarete von Falkensee

This is the delightfully wicked story of an era of infinite possibilities—especially when it comes to eroticism in all its bewitching forms. Among actors and aristocrats, with students and showgirls, in the cafes and salons, and at backstage parties in pleasure boudoirs, *Blue Angel Nights* describes the time when even the most outlandish proposal is likely to find an eager accomplice.

NOW AVAILABLE

Cybersex
Miranda Reigns

Collected for the first time in one volume is the entirety of Miranda Reigns's *Cyberwebs* trilogy. The trilogy follows Miranda, a young woman who indulges her darkest fantasies by plunging deep into the depths of the online erotic community. But, she soon finds that she cannot separate her online life from her real relationships. Riddled with guilt, Miranda attempts to untangle herself from these relationships, but finds that in the battle between morality and passion, it is the lascivious side of her that always wins.

Depravicus
Anonymous

The Reverend William Entercock is the highly unorthodox priest of Cumsdale Church. As well as running various lucrative undercover commercial enterprises the randy rev also enjoys distinctly worldly relationships with a range of the parish's young ladies, including the nuns. Bishop Simon Holesgood has his suspicions about the vivacious vicar. Joined by a vengeful Mother Superior, the Bishop sets out to get Entercock defrocked. Worse, an attractive young tabloid journalist wants to expose him for the sake of the sensational story that revelation of his excesses will make.

Sacred Exchange
Edited by Lisabet Sarai and S. F. Mayfair

Sacred Exchange is an anthology of original erotic fiction that explores the transcendent, spiritual, or magical aspects of the power exchange in Dominance and Submission. Through stories of ritual, communion, telepathy, devotion, dreams, commitment, and intense personal change, *Sacred Exchange* examines how the bond of trust between dominant and submissive can lead to emotional and spiritual revelations.

The Rooms
Michael Hemmingson

Danielle is the ultimate submissive, begging to do the nastiest, kinkiest acts for a Master. Two men, Alex and Gordon, have sexually enslaved her. They also happen to be her college professors. She opens the darkest regions of her slutty soul to them, revealing rooms of sexual adventure they never knew existed.

TITLES IN THE CAPTIVE SERIES

Available now

The Captive I, II
by Anonymous

Two classic tales of erotic enslavement, collected in a single volume for the first time

When a wealthy Englishman-about-town attempts to make advances on the beautiful twenty-year-old debutante Caroline Martin, she haughtily refuses him. As revenge, the wealthy man orders Caroline's abduction by the members of a white slavery ring who cater to the perverted desires of the aristocracy. Sequestered in a remote Moroccan mountain prison, Caroline begins an education in sexual submission that will prepare her for her real mentor.

Volume II recounts the history of Brigid, who has unwisely caused the prosecution of a wealthy admirer. As retribution, he has Brigid stolen away to the notorious Cambina Alta plantation. Naked and bound before the sadism of Colonel Mantrique and the perversities of the Comte de Xantra, Brigid endures the unyielding discipline of erotic enslavement until she is ready to welcome the master who has chosen her.

The Captive III, IV, V
by Richard Manton

Beauty lies in bondage everywhere in the tropical island of Cheluna where young girls are kept under the tight lock and key of the uncompromising masters of a white slavery ring. Collected here are three classic tales of pain and pleasure set on the shores of the notorious island.

In *Volume III*, two wealthy cousins venture deep beyond Cheluna to the remote settlement of Cambina Alta and a life of plantation discipline. *Volume IV*, follows the masked apprentice of Cheluna's master, whose mysterious and brutal ways catch the attention of Cheluna's girls. In *Volume V*, rebellious nineteen-year-old, Joanne is sent to Cheluna where she is taught the ways of the rod in preparation for a life of servitude at the palace home of the imperious Colonel Mantrique.

ORDER FORM

Attach a separate sheet for additional titles.

Title	Quantity	Price
______________________	____	______
______________________	____	______
______________________	____	______
______________________	____	______

Shipping and Handling (see charges below) ______

Sales tax (in CA and NY) ______

Total ______

Name ______________________

Address ______________________

City ______________ State ________ Zip ________

Daytime telephone number ______________________

❑ Check ❑ Money Order (US dollars only. No COD orders accepted.)

Credit Card # ______________________ Exp. Date ________

❑ MC ❑ VISA ❑ AMEX

Signature ______________________

(if paying with a credit card you must sign this form.)

Shipping and Handling charges:*

Domestic: $4 for 1st book, $.75 each additional book. International: $5 for 1st book, $1 each additional book

*rates in effect at time of publication. Subject to Change.

Mail order to Publishers Group West, Attention: Order Dept., 1700 Fourth St., Berkeley, CA 94710, or fax to (510) 528-3444.

PLEASE ALLOW 4-6 WEEKS FOR DELIVERY. ALL ORDERS SHIP VIA 4TH CLASS MAIL.

Look for Blue Moon Books at your favorite local bookseller or from your favorite online bookseller.